'Space Opera – the gran[...]
well, and in very good h[...]
work keeping and advancing the necessary forms and
traditions, expanding the discourse in a way that both
gladdens the heart and sends chills up the spines of
fellow writers.' *Greg Bear*

STEPHEN BAXTER
Reality Dust

The right of Stephen Baxter to be identified as the author
of this work has been asserted in accordance with the
Copyright, Designs and Patents Act of 1988.

This edition published in Great Britain in 2002 by

Gollancz
An imprint of the Orion Publishing Group
Orion House, 5 Upper St Martin's Lane,
London, WC2H 9EA

A CIP catalogue record for this book
is available from the British Library.

ISBN 0 575 07306 3

Typeset at The Spartan Press Ltd,
Lymington, Hants

Printed in Great Britain by
Clays Ltd, St Ives plc

An explosion of light: the moment of her birth.

She cried out.

A sense of self flooded through her body. She had arms, legs; her limbs were flailing. She was *falling*, and glaring light wheeled about her.

But she remembered another place: a black sky, a world – no, a *moon* – a face before her, smiling gently. *This won't hurt. Close your eyes.*

A name. *Callisto.*

But the memories were dissipating.

'No!'

She landed hard, face down, and she was suffused by sudden pain. Her face was pressed into dust, rough, gritty particles, each as big as a moon to her staring eyes.

The flitter rose from liberated Earth like a stone thrown from a blue bowl. The little cylindrical craft tumbled slowly as it climbed, sparkling, and Hama Druz marvelled at the beauty of the mist-laden, subtly curved landscape below him, drenched as it was in clear bright sunlight.

But the scars of the Occupation were still visible. Away

from the great Conurbations, much of the land still glistened silver-grey where starbreaker beams and Qax nanoreplicators had chewed up the surface of the Earth, life and rocks and all, turning it into a featureless silicate dust.

'But already,' he pointed out eagerly, 'life's green is returning. Look, Nomi, there, and there . . .'

His companion, Nomi Ferrer, grunted sceptically. 'But that greenery has nothing to do with edicts from your Interim Coalition of Governance, or all your philosophies. That's the worms, Hama, turning Qax dust back into soil. Just the worms, that's all.'

Hama would not be put off. Nomi, once a ragamuffin, was an officer in the Green Army, the most significant military force yet assembled in the wake of the departing Qax. She was forty years old, her body a solid slab of muscle, with burn marks disfiguring one cheek. And, in Hama's judgement, she was much too sunk in cynicism.

He slapped her on the shoulder. 'Quite right. And that's how *we* must be, Nomi: like humble worms, content to toil in the darkness, to turn a few scraps of our land back the way they should be. That should be enough for any life.'

Nomi just snorted.

The two-seat flitter began to descend towards a Conurbation. Still known by its Qax registration of 11729, the Conurbation was a broad, glistening sprawl of bubble-dwellings blown from the bedrock, and linked by the green-blue of umbilical canals. Hama saw that many of the dome-shaped buildings had been scarred by fire, some even cracked open. But the blue-green tetrahedral sigil of free Earth had been daubed on every surface.

A shadow passed over the Conurbation's glistening rooftops. Hama shielded his eyes and squinted upwards. A fleshy cloud briefly eclipsed the sun. It was a Spline ship: a living starship kilometres across, its hardened epidermis pocked with monitor and weapon emplacements. He suppressed a shudder. For generations the Spline had been the symbol of Qax dominance. But now the Qax had gone, and this last abandoned Spline was in the hands of human engineers, who sought to comprehend its strange biological workings.

On the outskirts of the Conurbation there was a broad pit scooped out of the ground, its crudely scraped walls denoting its origin as post-Occupation: human, not Qax. In this pit rested a number of silvery, insectile forms, and as the flitter fell further through the sunlit air, Hama could see people moving around the gleaming shapes, talking, working. The pit was a shipyard, operated by and for humans, who were slowly rediscovering yet another lost art; for no human engineer had built a spacecraft on Earth for three hundred years.

Hama pressed his face to the window – like a child, he knew, reinforcing Nomi's preconception of him – but to Lethe with self-consciousness. 'One of those ships is going to take us to Callisto. Imagine it, Nomi – a moon of Jupiter!'

But Nomi scowled. 'Just remember *why* we're going there: to hunt out jasofts – criminals and collaborators. It will be a grim business, Hama, no matter how pretty the scenery.'

The flitter slid easily through the final phases of its descent, and the domes of the Conurbation loomed around them.

There was a voice, talking fast, almost babbling.

'There is no time. There is no space. We live in a universe of static shapes. Do you see? Imagine a grain of dust that represents all the particles in *our* universe, frozen in time. Imagine a stupendous number of dust grains, representing all the possible shapes the particles can take. This is reality dust, a dust of the Nows. And the dust fills a realm of instants.' A snapping of fingers. 'There. There. There. Each moment, each juggling of the particles, a new grain. The reality dust contains all the arrangements of matter there could ever be. Reality dust is an image of eternity . . .'

She lay there, face pressed into the dirt, wishing none of this was happening.

Hands grabbed her, by shoulder and hip. She was dragged, flipped over on her back. The sky above was dazzling bright.

She cried out again.

A face loomed, silhouetted. She saw a hairless scalp, no eyebrows or lashes. The face itself was rounded, smoothed over, as if unformed. But she had a strong impression of great age.

'This won't hurt,' she whispered, terrified. 'Close your eyes.'

The face loomed closer. 'Nothing here is real.' The voice was harsh, without inflection. A man? 'Not even the dust.'

'Reality dust,' she murmured.

'Yes. Yes! It is reality dust. If you live, remember that.'

The face receded, turning away.

She tried to sit up. She pressed her hands into the loose dust, crushing low, crumbling structures, like the tunnels of worms. She glimpsed a flat horizon, a black, oily sea, forest-covered hills. She was on a beach, a beach of silvery, dusty sand. The sky was a glowing dome. The air was full of mist; she couldn't see very far, in any direction, as if she were trapped in a glowing bubble.

Her companion was mid-sized, his body shapeless and sexless. He was dressed in a coverall of a nondescript colour. He cast no shadow in the bright diffuse light.

She glanced down at herself. She was wearing a similar coverall. She fingered its smooth fabric, baffled.

He was walking slowly, limping, as though exhausted. Walking away, leaving her alone.

'Please,' she said.

Without stopping, he called back, 'If you stay there you'll die.'

'What's your name?'

'Pharaoh. That is all the name I have left, at any rate.'

She thought hard. Those sharp birth memories had fled, but still . . . '*Callisto*. My name is Callisto.'

Pharaoh laughed. 'Of course it is.'

Without warning, pain swamped her right hand.

She snatched it to her chest. The skin felt as if it had been drenched in acid.

The sea had risen, she saw, and the black, lapping fluid had covered her hand. Where the fluid had touched, the flesh was flaking away, turning to chaotic dust, exposing sketchy bones that crumbled and fell in thin slivers.

She screamed. She had only been here a moment, and already such a terrible thing had happened.

Pharaoh limped back to her. 'Think beyond the pain.'

'I can't –'

'*Think*. There is no pain.'

And, as he said it, she realised it was true. Her hand was *gone*, her arm terminating in a smooth, rounded stump. But it didn't hurt. How could that be?

'What do you feel?'

'. . . Diminished,' she said.

'Good,' he said. 'You're learning. There is no pain here. Only forgetting.'

The black, sticky fluid was lapping near her legs. She scrambled away. But when she tried to use her missing right hand she stumbled, falling flat.

Pharaoh locked his hand under her arm and hauled her to her feet. The brief exertion seemed to exhaust him; his face smoothed further, as if blurring. 'Go,' he said.

'Where?'

'Away from the sea.' And he pushed her, feebly, away from the ocean.

She looked that way doubtfully. The beach sloped upward sharply; it would be a difficult climb. Above the beach there was what looked like a forest, tall shapes like trees, a carpet of something like grass. She saw people moving in the darkness between the trees. But the forest was dense, a place of colourless, flat shadows, made grey by the mist.

She looked back. Pharaoh was standing where she had left him, a pale, smoothed-over figure just a few paces from the lapping, encroaching sea, already dimmed by the thick white mist.

She called, 'Aren't you coming?'

'Go.'

'I'm afraid.'

'Asgard. Help her.'

Callisto turned. There was a woman, not far away, crawling over the beach. She seemed to be plucking stray grass blades from the dust, cramming them into her mouth. Her face was a mask of wrinkles, complex, textured – a stark contrast to Pharaoh's smoothed-over countenance. Her voice querulous, she snapped, 'Why should I?'

'Because I once helped you.'

The woman got to her feet, growling.

Callisto quailed. But Asgard took her good hand and began to haul her up the beach.

Callisto looked back once more. The oil-black sea lapped thickly over a flat, empty beach. Pharaoh had gone.

As they made their way to Hama's assigned office, Nomi drew closer to Hama's side, keeping her weapons obvious.

The narrow corridors of Conurbation 11729 were grievously damaged by fire and weaponry – and they were scars inflicted not by Qax, but by humans. In some places there was even a smell of burning.

And the corridors were crowded: not just with former inhabitants of the Qax-built city, but with others Hama couldn't help but think of as *outsiders*.

There were ragamuffins – like Nomi herself – the product of generations who had waited out the Occupation in the ruins of ancient human cities, and other corners of wilderness Earth. And there were returned refugees and traders, the descendants of people who had fled to the outer moons and even beyond the Solar System to escape the Qax's powerful, if inefficient, grasp. Some of these returned space travellers were exotic indeed, with skin darkened by the light of other stars, and frames made spindly or squat by other gravities – even eyes replaced by Eyes, mechanical supplements. And most of them had *hair*: hair sprouting wildly from their heads and even their faces, in colours of varying degrees of outrage. They made the Conurbation's Occupation-era inhabitants, with their drab monkish robes and shaven heads, look like characterless drones.

The various factions eyed each other with suspicion, even hostility; Hama saw no signs of unity among liberated mankind.

Hama's office turned out to be a spacious room, the walls lined with data slates. It even had a natural-light window, overlooking a swathe of the Conurbation and the lands beyond.

This prestigious room had once, of course, been assigned to a jasoft – a human collaborator administering Earth on behalf of the Qax – and Hama felt a deep reluctance to enter it. For Hama, up to now, the libera-

tion had been painless, a time of opportunity and freedom, like a wonderful game. But that, he knew, was
about to change.

Hama Druz, twenty-five years old, had been assigned
to the Commission for Historical Truth, the tribunal
appointed to investigate and try collaboration crimes.
His job was to hunt out jasofts.

Some of these collaborators were said to be *pharaohs*,
kept alive by Qax technology, perhaps for centuries . . .
Some, it was said, were even survivors of the pre-
Occupation period, when human science had advanced
enough to beat back death. If the jasofts were hated, the
pharaohs had been despised most of all; for the longer
they had lived, the more loyalty they owed to the Qax,
and the more effectively they administered the Qax
regime. And that regime had become especially brutal
after a flawed human Rebellion more than a century
earlier.

Hama, accompanied by Nomi, would spend a few days
here, acquainting himself with the issues around the
collaborators. But to complete his assignment he would
have to travel far beyond the Earth: to Jupiter's moon,
Callisto, in fact. There – according to records kept during
the Occupation by the jasofts themselves – a number of
pharaohs had fled to a science station maintained by one
of their number, a man named Reth Cana.

For the next few days Hama worked through the data
slates assembled for him, and received visitors, petitions,
claimants. He quickly learned that there were many
issues here beyond the crimes of the collaborator class.

The Conurbation itself faced endless problems day to day. The Conurbations had been deliberately designed by the Qax as temporary cities. It was all part of the grand strategy of the latter Occupation; the Qax's human subjects were not to be allowed ties of family, of home, of loyalty to anybody or anything – except perhaps the Occupation itself.

The practical result was that the hastily-constructed Conurbation was quickly running down. Hama read gloomily through report after report of silting-up canals and failing heating or lighting and crumbling dwelling-places. There were people sickening of diseases long thought vanished from the planet – even hunger had returned.

And then there were the wars.

The aftermath of the Qax's withdrawal – the overnight removal of the government of Earth after three centuries – had been extremely difficult. In less than a month humans had begun fighting humans once more. It had taken a chaotic half-year before the Interim Coalition had coalesced, and even now, around the planet, brushfire battles still raged against warlords armed with Qax weaponry.

And it had been the jasofts, of course, who had been the focus of the worst conflicts. In many places jasofts, including pharaohs, had been summarily executed. Else-where the jasofts had gone into hiding, or fled off-world, or had even fought back.

The Interim Coalition had quelled the bloodshed by promising that the collaborators would be brought to justice before the new Commission for Historical Truth. But Hama – alone in his office, poring over his data slates – knew that justice was easier promised than delivered. How were short-lived humans – dismissively called *mayflies* by the pharaohs – to try crimes whose commission might date back centuries? There were no witnesses save the pharaohs themselves; no formal records save those maintained under the Occupation; no testimony save a handful of legends preserved through the endless dissolutions of the Conurbations; not even any physical evidence since the Qax's great Extirpation had wiped the Earth clean of its past.

What made it even more difficult, Hama was slowly discovering, was that the jasofts were *useful*.

It was a matter of compromise, of practical politics. The jasofts knew how the world worked, on the mundane level of keeping people alive, for they had administered the planet for centuries. So some jasofts – offered amnesties for cooperating – were discreetly running parts of Earth's new, slowly-coalescing administration, just as they had under the Qax.

And meanwhile, children were going hungry.

Hama had, subtly, protested against his new assignment.

He felt his strength lay in philosophy, in abstraction. He longed to rejoin the debates going on in great constitutional conventions all over the planet, as the human race, newly liberated from the Qax, sought a new way to govern itself.

But his appeal against reassignment had been turned

down. There was simply too much to do *now*, too great a mess to clear up, and too few able and trustworthy people available to do it.

It was so bad, in fact, that some people were openly calling for the return of the Qax. *At least we were kept warm and fed under the Qax. At least there were no bandits trying to rob or kill us. And there were none of these disgusting ragamuffins cluttering up the public places . . .*

As he witnessed the clamour of the crowds around the failing food dispensers, Hama felt a deep horror – and a determination that this should not recur. And yet, to his shame, he looked forward to escaping from all this complexity to the cool open spaces of the Jovian system.

It was while he was in this uncertain mood that the pharaoh sought him out.

Asgard led her to the fringe of the forest. There, ignoring Callisto, she hunkered down and began to pull at strands of grass, ripping them from the ground and pushing them into her mouth.

Callisto watched doubtfully. 'What should I do?'

Asgard shrugged. 'Eat.'

Reluctantly, Callisto got to her knees. Favouring her truncated arm, it was difficult to keep her balance. With her left hand she pulled a few blades of the grass stuff from the dust. She crammed the grass into her mouth and chewed. It was moist, tasteless, slippery.

She found that the grass blades weren't connected to roots. Rather they seemed to blend back into the dust, to the tube-like structures there. Deeper into the forest's gathering darkness the grass grew longer, plaiting itself into ropy vine-like plants. And deeper still she saw things like trees looming tall.

People moved among the trees, digging at the roots with their bare hands, pushing fragments of food into their faces.

'My name,' she said, 'is Callisto.'

Asgard grunted. 'Your dream-name.'

'I remembered it.'

'No, you *dreamed*.'

'What is this place?'

'It isn't a place.'

'What's it called?'

'It has no name.' Asgard held up a blade of grass. 'What colour is this?'

'Green,' Callisto said immediately . . . but that wasn't true. It wasn't green. What colour, then? She realised she couldn't say.

Asgard laughed, and shoved the blade in her mouth.

Callisto looked down the beach. 'What happened to Pharaoh?'

Asgard shrugged. 'He might be dead by now. Washed away by the sea.'

'Why doesn't he come up here, where it's safe?'

'Because he's weak. Weak and mad.'

'He saved me from the sea.'

'He helps all the newborns.'

'Why?'

'How should I know? But it's futile. The ocean rises and falls. Every time it comes a little closer, higher up the beach. Soon it will lap right up here, to the forest itself.'

'We'll have to go into the forest.'

'Try that and Night will kill you.'

Night? Callisto looked into the forest's darkness, and shuddered.

Asgard eyed Callisto with curiosity, no sympathy. 'You really are a newborn, aren't you?' She dug her hand into the dust, shook it until a few grains were left on her palm. 'You know what the first thing Pharaoh said to *me* was? "Nothing is real." '

'Yes –'

' "Not even the dust. *Because every grain is a whole world.*" ' She looked up at Callisto, calculating.

Callisto gazed at the sparkling grains, wondering, baffled, frightened.

Too much strangeness.

I want to go home, she thought desperately. But where, and what, is home?

Two women walked into Hama's office: one short, squat, her face a hard mask, and the other apparently younger, taller, willowy. They both wore bland, rather scuffed Occupation-era robes – as he did – and their heads were shaven bare.

The older woman met his gaze steadily. 'My name is Gemo Cana. This is my daughter. She is called Sarfi.'

Hama eyed them with brief curiosity.

This was a routine appointment. Gemo Cana was, supposedly, a representative of a citizens' group concerned about details of the testimony being heard by the preliminary hearings of the Truth Commission. The archaic words of family – *daughter, mother* – were still strange to Hama, but they were becoming increasingly more common, as the era of the Qax cadres faded from memory.

The daughter, Sarfi, averted her eyes. She looked very young, and her face was thin, her skin sallow.

He welcomed them with his standard opening remarks. 'My name is Hama Druz. I am an advisor to the Interim Coalition and specifically to the Commission for Historical Truth. I will listen to whatever you wish to tell me and will help you any way I can; but you must understand that my role here is not formal, and –'

'You're tired,' Gemo Cana said.

'What?'

She stepped forward and studied him, her gaze direct, disconcerting. 'It's harder than you thought, isn't it? Running an office, a city – a world. Especially as you must work by persuasion, consent.' She walked around the room, ran a finger over the data slates fixed on the walls, and paused before the window, gazing out at the glistening rooftops of the Conurbation, the muddy blue-green of the canals. Hama could see the Spline ship rolling in the sky, a wrinkled moon. She said, 'It was difficult enough in the era of the Qax, whose authority, backed by Spline gunships, was unquestionable.'

'And,' asked Hama, 'how exactly do you know that?'

'This used to be my office.'

Hama reached immediately for his desktop.

'Please.' The girl, Sarfi, reached out towards him, then seemed to think better of it. 'Don't call your guards. Hear us out.'

He stood. 'You're a jasoft, Gemo Cana.'

'Oh, worse than that,' Gemo murmured. 'I'm a *pharaoh* . . . You know, I have missed this view. The Qax knew what they were doing when they gave us jasofts the sunlight.'

She was the first pharaoh Hama had encountered face to face. Hama quailed before her easy authority, her sense of dusty age; he felt young, foolish, his precious philosophies half-formed. And he found himself staring at the girl; he hadn't even known pharaohs could have children.

Deliberately he looked away, seeking a way to regain control of the situation. 'You've been in hiding.'

Gemo inclined her head. 'I spent a long time in this office, Hama Druz. Longer than you can imagine. I always knew the day would come when the Qax would leave us exposed.'

'So you prepared.'

'Wouldn't you? I was doing my duty. I didn't want to die for it.'

'Your duty to Qax occupiers?'

'No,' she said, a note of weariness in her voice. 'You seem more intelligent than the rest; I had hoped you might understand that much. It was a duty to mankind, of course. It always was.'

He tapped a data slate on his desk. '*Gemo Cana*. I should have recognised the name. You are one of the most hunted jasofts. Your testimony before the Commission –'

She snapped, 'I'm not here to surrender, Hama Druz, but to ask for your help.'

'I don't understand.'

'I know about your mission to Callisto. To the enclave there. Reth has been running a science station since before the Occupation. Now *you* are going out there to close him down.'

He said grimly, 'These last few years have not been a time for science.'

She nodded. 'So you believe science is a luxury, a plaything for easier times. But science is a thread in the tapestry of our humanity – a thread Reth has maintained. Do you even know what he is doing out there?'

'Something to do with life forms in the ice –'

'Oh, much more than that. Reth has been exploring the nature of reality – *seeking a way to abolish time itself.*' She smiled coolly. 'I don't expect you to understand. But it has been a fitting goal, in an era when the Qax have sought to obliterate human history – to abolish the passage of time from the human consciousness . . .'

He frowned. *Abolishing time?* Such notions were strange to him, meaningless. He said, 'We have evidence that the science performed on Callisto was only a cover – that many pharaohs fled there during the chaotic period following the Qax withdrawal.'

'Only a handful. There only ever was a handful of us, you know. And now that some have achieved a more fundamental escape, into death, there are fewer than ever.'

'What do you *want*?'

'I want you to take us there.'

'To Callisto?'

'We will remain in your custody, you and your guards. You may restrain us as you like. We will not try anything – *heroic*. All we want is sanctuary. They will kill us, you see.'

'The Commission is not a mob.'

She ignored that. 'I am not concerned for myself, but for my daughter. Sarfi has nothing to do with this; she is no jasoft.'

'Then she will not be harmed.'

Gemo just laughed.

'You are evading justice, Gemo Cana.'

She leaned forward, resting her hands on the desk nonchalantly; this really had been her office, he realised. '*There is no justice here*,' she hissed. 'How can there be? I am asking you to spare my daughter's life. Later, I will gladly return to face whatever inquisition you choose to set up.'

'Why would this *Reth* help you?'

'His name is Reth Cana,' she said. 'He is my brother. Do you understand? Not my cadre sibling. My *brother*.'

Gemo Cana; Reth Cana.

In the Qax world, families had been a thing for ragamuffins and refugees, and human names had become arbitrary labels; the coincidence of names had meant nothing to Hama. But to these ancient survivors, a shared name was a badge of kinship. He glanced at Gemo and Sarfi, uneasy in the presence of these close primitive ties, of mother and brother and daughter.

Abruptly the door opened; Nomi Ferrer walked in, reading from a data slate. 'Hama, your ship is ready to go. But I think we have to . . .' She looked up, took in the scene at a glance. In an instant she was at Gemo's side, with a laser pistol pressed against the pharaoh's throat. 'Gemo Cana,' she hissed. 'How did you get in here?'

Sarfi stepped towards Nomi, hands fluttering like birds.

Hama held up his hand. 'Nomi, wait.'

Nomi was angered. 'Wait for what? Standing orders, Hama. This is a Category One jasoft who hasn't presented herself to the Commission. I should already have killed her.'

Gemo smiled thinly. 'It isn't so easy, is it, Hama Druz? You can theorise all you want about justice and retribution. But here in this office, you must confront the reality of a mother and her child.'

Sarfi said to Hama, 'If your guard kills my mother, she kills me too.'

'No,' said Hama. 'We aren't barbarians. You have nothing to fear –'

Sarfi reached out and swept her arm down at the desk – no, Hama saw, startled; her arm passed *through* the desk, briefly breaking up into a cloud of pixels, boxes of glowing colour.

'You're a Virtual,' he whispered.

'Yes. And do you want to know where *I* live?' She stepped up to her mother and pushed her hand into Gemo's skull.

Gemo observed his lack of comprehension. 'You don't

know much about us, do you, even though you presume to judge us? . . . Hama, pharaohs do not breed true.'

'Your daughter was mortal?'

'The Qax's gift was ambiguous. We watched our children grow old and die. *That* was our reward for serving the Qax; perhaps your Commission will accept *that* historical truth. And when she died –'

'When she died, you downloaded her into your *head*?'

'Nowhere else was safe,' Gemo said. 'And I was glad to, umm, make room for her. I have lived a long time; there were memories I was happy to shed . . .'

Nomi said harshly, 'But she isn't your daughter. She's a copy.'

Gemo closed her eyes. 'But she's all I have left.'

Sarfi looked away, as if ashamed.

Hama felt moved, and repelled, by this act of obsessive love.

There was a low concussion. The floor shuddered.

Nomi Ferrer understood immediately. 'Lethe. That was an explosion.'

Hama could hear running footsteps, cries. The light dropped, as if some immense shadow were passing over the sky. Hama ran to the window.

All around the Conurbation, ships were lifting, hauled into the sky by silent Qax technology, an eerie rising of ballooning metal flanks. But they entered a sky that was already crowded, darkened by the rolling, meaty bulk of a Spline craft.

Hama quailed from the brute physical reality of the erupting conflict. And he knew who to blame. 'It's the jasofts,' he said. 'The ones taken to orbit to help with the salvaging of the Spline. They took it over. And now they've come here, to rescue their colleagues . . .'

Gemo smiled, squinting up at the sky. 'Sadly, stupidity is not the sole prerogative of mayflies. This counter-coup cannot succeed. And then, when this Spline no longer darkens the sky, your vengeance will not be moderated by show trials and bleats about justice and truth . . .'

Sarfi pressed her hands to her face.

Hama stared at Gemo. '*You knew*. You knew this was about to happen. You timed your visit to force me to act.'

'It's all very complicated, Hama Druz,' Gemo said softly, manipulating. 'Don't you think so? Get us out of here – all of us – and sort it out later.'

Nomi pulled back the pharaoh's head. 'You know what I think? I think you're a monster, pharaoh. I think you killed your daughter, long ago, and stuck her in your head. An insurance against a day like today.'

Gemo, her face twisted by Nomi's strong fingers, forced a smile. 'Even if that were true, what difference would it make?' And she gazed at Hama, waiting for his decision.

Obeying Nomi's stern voice commands, the ship rose sharply. Hama felt nothing as shadows slipped over his lap.

This small craft, commissioned to take Hama to Jupiter's moons, was little more than a translucent hemisphere. In fact it would serve as a lifedome, part of a greater structure waiting in Earth orbit to propel him across the Solar System. The three of them, plus Sarfi, were jammed into a cabin made for two. The Virtual girl was forced to share the space already occupied by Hama and Gemo. Where her projection intersected their bodies it dimmed and broke up, and she averted her face; Hama was embarrassed by this brutal indignity.

The ship emerged from its pit and rushed beneath the looming belly of the Spline; there was a brief, ugly moment of fleeing, crumpled flesh, oozing scars metres long, glistening weapon emplacements dug in like stab wounds.

The air was crowded. Ships of all sizes cruised above Conurbation 11729, seeking to engage the Spline. Hama saw, with a sinking heart, that one of the ancient, half-salvaged ships had crashed back to Earth. It had made a broad crater, a wound in the ground circled by burning blown-silicate buildings. Already people had died today, irreplaceable lives lost forever.

The ship reached clear sky and soared upward. Earth folded over into a glowing blue abstraction, pointlessly beautiful, hiding the gruesome scenes below; the air thinned, the sky dimming through violet, to black.

The lifedome began to seek out the orbiting angular structure that would carry it to the outer planets.

Hama began to relax, for the first time since Gemo had revealed herself. Despite everything that had happened he was relieved to leave behind the complication of the Conurbation; perhaps in the thin light of Jupiter the dilemmas he would have to face would be simpler.

Sarfi gasped.

A vast winged shape sailed over the blue hide of Earth, silent, like a predator.

Hama's heart sank at the sight of this new, unexpected intruder. What now?

Nomi said softly, 'Those wings must be hundreds of kilometres across.'

'Ah,' said Gemo. 'Just like the old stories. The ship *is* like a sycamore seed . . . But none of you remembers *sycamore trees*, do you? Perhaps you need us, and our memories, after all.'

Nomi said, anger erupting, 'People are dying down there because of your kind, Gemo –'

Hama placed a hand on her arm. 'Tell us, pharaoh. Is it Qax?'

'Not Qax,' she said. '*Xeelee*.' It was the first time Hama had heard the name. 'That is a Xeelee nightfighter,' said Gemo. 'The question is – what does it want here?'

There was a soft warning chime.

The ship shot away from Earth. The planet dwindled, closing on itself, becoming a sparkling blue bauble, a bauble over which a black-winged insect crawled.

Callisto joined the community of foragers.

Dwelling where the forest met the beach, the people ate the grass, and sometimes leaves from the lower branches, even loose flaps of bark. The people were wary, solitary. She didn't learn their names – if they had any – nor gained a clear impression of their faces, their sexes. She wasn't even sure how many of them there were here.

Not many, she thought.

Callisto found herself eating incessantly. With every mouthful she took she felt herself grow, subtly, in some invisible direction – the opposite to the diminution she had suffered when she lost her hand to the burning power of the sea. There was nothing to drink – no fluid save the oily black ink of the ocean, and she wasn't tempted to try that. But it didn't seem to matter.

Callisto was not without curiosity.

The beach curved away, in either direction. Perhaps this was an island, poking out of the looming black ocean.

There was no bedrock, not as far as she could dig. Only the drifting, uniform dust.

There were structures in the dust: crude tubes and trails, like the markings of worms or crabs. The grass *emerged*, somehow, coalescing from looser dust formations. The grass grew sparsely on the open beach, but at the fringe of the forest it gathered in dense clumps. In some tufts the long blades wove together until they merged, forming more substantial, ropy plants.

Tiring of Asgard's cold company, she plucked up her courage and walked away from the beach, deeper into the forest.

Away from the lapping of the sea and the wordless rustle of the foraging people, it grew dark, quiet. Grass ropes wrapped around her legs, tugging, yielding with reluctance as she passed. This was a drab, still, lifeless place, she thought. In bush like this there ought to be texture: movement, noise, scent. So, anyhow, her flawed memories dimly protested.

She found a thick, solid mass, like a tree root. It was a tangle of grassy ropes, melding into a more substantial whole. She followed it. The root soon twined around another, and then another, the whole soon merging into a snaking cylinder broad enough to walk on. And from all around her more such giant roots were converging, as if she were approaching some great confluence of life.

At last the roots left the ground before her and rose up in a thick, twisted tangle, impossible to penetrate.

She peered up. The root stems coalesced into a thick unified trunk. It was a 'tree' that rose above the surrounding vegetative mass and into the light of the sky. But a low mist lay heavily, obscuring her view of the tree's upper branches.

She felt curiosity spark.

She placed her hand on the knotted-up lower trunk, then one foot, and then the other. The stuff of the tree was hard and cold.

At first the climbing was easy, the components of the 'trunk' loosely separated. She found a way to lodge her bad arm in gaps in the trunk so she could release her left hand briefly, and grab for a new handhold before she fell back. But as she climbed higher the ropy sub-trunks grew ever more tangled.

High above her the trunk soared upwards, daunting, disappearing into the mist. But she thought she made out branches arching through the mist, high above the surrounding vegetation. When she looked down, she saw how the 'roots' of this great structure dispersed over the forest floor, branching into narrower trees and vine-thin creepers and at last clumps of grass, dispersing into the underlying dust. She felt unexpectedly exhilarated by this small adventure –

There was a snarl, of greed and anger. It came from just above her head.

She quailed, slipped. She finished up dangling by her one hand.

It was human. Or, it might once have been human. It must have been four, five times her size. It was naked, and it clung to the tree above her, upside down, so that a broad face leered, predator's eyes fixed on her. Its limbs were cylinders of muscle, its chest and bulging belly massive, weighty. And it was male: an erection poked crudely between its legs.

It thrust its mouth at her, hissing. She could smell blood on its breath.

She screamed and lost her grip.

She fell, sliding down the trunk. She scrabbled for purchase with her feet and her one good hand. She slammed repeatedly against the trunk, and the wind was knocked out of her.

Above her, the beast receded, still staring into her eyes.

When she reached the ground, ignoring the aches of battered body and torn feet, she blundered away, running until she reached the openness of the beach.

For an unmeasured time she lay on the beach, drawing comfort from the graininess of the dust.

The craft was called a GUTship.

As finally assembled, it looked something like a parasol

of iron and ice. The canopy of the parasol was the habitable lifedome, and the 'handle' was the GUTdrive unit itself, embedded in a block of asteroid ice which served as reaction mass. The shaft of the parasol, separating the lifedome from the drive unit, was a kilometre-long spine of metal bristling with antennae and sensors.

The design was centuries old.

The ship itself had been built long before the Occupation, and lovingly maintained by a colony of refugees who had seen out the Qax era huddled in the asteroid belt. In a hundred subtle ways the ship showed its age. Every surface in the lifedome was scuffed and polished from use, the soft coverings of chairs and bunks were extensively patched, and many of the major systems bore the scars of rebuilding.

GUT, it seemed, was an acronym for Grand Unified Theory. Once, Gemo whispered, unified-theory energy had fuelled the expansion of the universe itself. In the heart of each GUTdrive asteroid ice was compressed to conditions resembling the initial singularity – the Big Bang. There, the fundamental forces governing the structure of matter merged into a single superforce. When the matter was allowed to expand again, the phase energy of the decomposing superforce, released like heat from condensing steam, was used to expel asteroid matter as a vapour rocket . . .

Remarkable, exotic, strange; this might be a primitive ship compared to a mighty Spline vessel, but Hama had never dreamed that mere humans had once mastered such technologies.

But when they were underway, with the lifedome opaqued over and all the strangeness shut out, none of that mattered. To Hama it was like being back in the Conurbations, in the enclosed, claustrophobic days before the Occupation was lifted. A deep part of his mind seemed to believe that what lay beyond these walls – occupied Earth, or endless universe – did not matter so long as *he* was safe and warm. He felt comfortable in his mobile prison – and was guilty to feel that way.

But everything changed when they reached Callisto.

They entered a wide, slow orbit around the ice moon.

The sun was shrunk to the tiniest of discs by Jupiter's remoteness, five times as far as Earth from the central light. When Hama held up his hand it cast sharp, straight shadows, the shadows of infinity, and he felt no warmth.

And through this rectilinear, reduced light, Callisto swam.

The satellite was like a dark, misty twin of Earth's Moon. Its surface was crowded with craters – even more so than the Moon's, for there were none of the giant lava-flood seas that smoothed over much lunar terrain. The largest craters were complex structures, plains of pale ice surrounded by multiple arcs of folded and cracked land, like ripples frozen into shattered ice and rock. Some of these features were the size of continents, large enough to stretch around this lonely moon's curved horizon, evidently the results of immense, terrifying impacts.

But these great geological sculptures were oddly

smoothed out, the cracks and ripples reduced to shallow ridges. Unlike the rocky Moon, Callisto was made of rock and water ice. Over billions of years the ice had suffered viscous relaxation; it flowed and slumped. The most ancient craters had simply subsided, like great geological sighs, leaving these spectacular palimpsests.

'The largest impact structure is called Valhalla,' Gemo was saying. 'Once there were human settlements all along the northern faces of the circular ridges. All dark now, of course – save where Reth has made his base.'

Nomi grunted, uninterested in tourism. 'Then that's where we land.'

Hama gazed out at this silent sculpture of ice and time. 'Remarkable,' he said. 'I never imagined –'

Gemo said caustically, 'You are a drone of the Occupation. You never even saw the sunlight, you never imagined a universe beyond the walls of your Conurbation, you have never lived. You have no *memory*. And yet you presume to judge. Do you even know why Callisto is so-called? It is an ancient myth. Callisto was a nymph, beloved of Zeus and hated by jealous Hera, who metamorphosed her into a bear . . .' She seemed to sense Hama's bafflement. 'Ah, but you don't even remember the *Gree-chs*, do you?'

Nomi confronted her. '*You* administered the Extirpation, pharaoh. Your arrogance over the memories you took from us is –'

'Ill-mannered,' Hama said smoothly, and he touched Nomi's shoulder, seeking to calm the situation. 'A lack of grace that invalidates her assumption of superiority over us. Don't concern yourself, Nomi. She condemns herself and her kind every time she speaks.'

Gemo glared at him, full of contempt.

But now Jupiter rose.

The four of them crowded to see. They bobbed in the air like balloons, thrust into weightlessness now the drive was shut down.

The largest of planets was a dish of muddy light, of cloudy bands, pink and purple and brown. Where the bands met, Hama could see fine lines of turbulence, swoops and swirls like a lunatic water-colour. But a single vast storm disfigured those smooth bands, twisting and stirring them right across the southern hemisphere of the planet, as if the whole of Jupiter were being sucked into some vast central maw.

As perhaps it was. There was a legend that, a century before, human rebels called the Friends of Wigner had climaxed their revolt by escaping *back through time*, across thousands of years, and had hurled a black hole into the heart of Jupiter. The knot of compressed spacetime was already distorting Jupiter's immense, dreamy structure, and in perhaps a million years would destroy the great world altogether. It was a fantastic story, probably no more than a tale spun for comfort during the darkest hours of Occupation.

Still, it was clear that *something* was wrong with Jupiter. Nobody knew the truth – except perhaps the pharaohs, and they would say nothing.

Hama saw how Sarfi, entranced, tried to rest her hand against the lifedome's smooth transparency. But her hand sank into the surface, crumbling, and she snatched it away quickly. Such incidents seemed to cause Sarfi deep distress – as if she had been programmed with deep taboos about violating the physical laws governing 'real' humans. Perhaps it even hurt her when such breaches occurred.

Gemo Cana did not appear to notice her daughter's pain.

The lifedome neatly detached itself from the ship's drive section and swept smoothly down from orbit. Hama watched the moon's folded-over, crater-starred landscape flatten out, the great circular ramparts of Valhalla marching over the close horizon.

The lifedome settled to the ice with the gentlest of crunches.

A walkway extended from a darkened building block, and nuzzled hesitantly against the ship. A hatch sighed open.

Hama stood in the hatchway. The walkway was a transparent, shimmering tube before him, concealing little of the silver-black morphology of the collapsed landscape beyond. The main feature was the big Valhalla ridge, of course. Seen this close it was merely a rise in the land, a scarp that marched to either horizon: it would have been impossible to tell from the ground that this was in fact part of a great circular rampart surrounding a continent-sized impact scar, and Hama felt insignificant, dwarfed.

He forced himself to take the first step along the walkway.

The gravity here was about an eighth of Earth's,

comparable to the Moon's, and to walk through Callisto's crystal stillness was enchanting; he floated between footsteps in great bounds.

Gemo mocked his pleasure. 'We are like *Armm-stron* and *All-dinn*.'

Nomi growled, 'More *Gree-chs*, pharaoh?'

Reth Cana was waiting to meet them at the end of the walkway.

He was short, squat, with a crisp scalp of white hair, and he wore a practical-looking coverall of some papery fabric. He was scowling at them, his face a round wrinkled mask.

Beyond him, Hama glimpsed extensive chambers, dug into the ice, dimly lit by a handful of floating globe lamps – extensive, but deserted.

But Hama's gaze was drawn back to Reth. *He looks like Gemo*.

Gemo stepped forward now, and they faced each other, brother and sister separated for centuries. Stiffly, they embraced. They were like copies of each other, subtly morphed.

Sarfi hung back, watching, hands folded before her.

Hama felt excluded, almost envious of this piece of complex humanity. How must it be to be bound to another person by such strong ties – for life?

Reth stepped away from his sister and inspected Sarfi. Without warning he swept his clenched fist through the girl's belly. He made a trail of disrupted pixels, like a fleshy comet. Sarfi crumpled over, crying out.

The sudden brutality shocked Hama.

Reth laughed. 'A Virtual? I didn't suspect you were so sentimental, Gemo.'

Gemo stepped forward, her mouth working. 'But I remember your cruelty.'

Now Reth faced Hama. 'And this is the one sent by Earth's new junta of children.'

Hama shrank before Reth's arrogance and authority. His accent was exotic – antique, perhaps; there was a rustle of history about this man. Hama tried to keep his voice steady. 'I have a specific assignment here, sir –'

Reth snorted. 'My work, a project of centuries, deals with the essence of reality itself. It is an achievement of which you have *no* understanding. If you had a glimmer of sensitivity you would leave now. Just as, if you and your mayfly friends had any true notion of duty, you would abandon your petty attempts at governing.'

Nomi growled. 'You think we got rid of the Qax just to hand over our lives to the likes of you?'

Reth glared at her. 'Can you really believe that *we* would have administered the withdrawal of the Qax with more death and destruction than *you* have inflicted?'

Hama stood straight. 'I'm not here to discuss hypotheticals with you, Reth Cana. We are pragmatic. If your work is in the interest of the species –'

Reth laughed out loud; Hama saw how his teeth were discoloured, greenish. '*The interest of the species.*' He stalked about the echoing cavern, posturing. 'Gemo, I give you the future. If this young man has his way, science will be no more than a weapon! . . . And if I refuse to cooperate with his *pragmatism*?'

Nomi said smoothly, 'Those who follow us will be a lot tougher. Believe it, jasoft.'

Gemo listened, stony-faced.

'Tomorrow,' Reth said to Hama. 'Twelve hours from now. I will demonstrate my work, my results. But I will not justify it to the likes of you; make of it what you will.' And he swept away into shadows beyond the fitful glow of the hovering globe lamps.

Nomi said quietly to Hama, 'Reth is a man who has spent too long alone.'

'We can deal with him,' Hama said with more confidence than he felt.

'Perhaps. But *why* is he alone? Hama, we know that at least a dozen pharaohs came to this settlement before the Occupation was ended, and probably more during the collapse. Where are *they*?'

Hama frowned. 'Find out.'

Nomi nodded briskly.

The oily sea lapped even closer now. The beach was reduced to a thin strip, trapped between forest and sea.

She walked far along the beach. There was nothing different, just the same dense forest, the oily sea. Here and there the sea had already covered the beach, encroaching into the forest, and she had to push into the vegetation to make further progress. Everywhere she found the tangle of roots and vine-like growths. Where the rising liquid had touched, the grasses and vines and trees crumbled and died, leaving bare, scattered dust.

The beach curved around on itself.

She was on an island. At least she had learned that much. Eventually, she supposed, that dark sea would rise so high it would cover everything. And they would all die.

There was no night. When she was tired, she rested on the beach, eyes closed.

There was no time here – not in the way she seemed to remember, on some deep level of herself: no days, no nights, no change. There was only the beach, the forest, that black oily sea, lapping ever closer, all of it under a shadowless grey-white sky.

She looked inward, seeking herself. She found only fragments of memory: an ice moon, a black sky – a face, a girl's perhaps, delicate, troubled. She didn't like to think about the face. It made her feel – complex. Lonely. Guilty.

She asked Asgard about time.

Asgard, gnawing absently on a handful of bark chips, ran a casual finger through the reality dust, from grain to grain. 'There,' she said. 'Time passing. From one moment to the next. For we, you see, are above time.'

'I don't understand.'

'Of course you don't. A blade of grass is a shard of story. Where the grass knits itself into vines and trees, that story deepens. And if *I* eat a grass blade I absorb its tiny story, and it becomes mine. So Pharaoh said. And I don't know who told *him*. Do you see?'

'No,' said Callisto frankly.

Asgard just looked at her, apathetic, contemptuous.

There was a thin cry, from the ocean. Callisto shaded her eyes, looked that way.

It had been a newborn, thrust arbitrarily into the air, just as Callisto had been. But this newborn had fallen, not to the comparative safety of the dust, but direct into the sea. She – or he – made barely a ripple on that placid black surface. Callisto saw a hand raised briefly above the sluggish meniscus, the flesh already dissolving, white bones curling.

And then it was gone, the newborn lost.

Callisto felt a deep horror.

Now, as she looked along the beach, she saw dark masses – a mound of flesh, the grisly articulation of fingers – fragments of the suddenly dead, washed up on this desolate beach. This had happened before, she realised. Over and over.

Asgard sat apathetically, chewing on her bark.

Is this it? Callisto wondered. Must I sit here like Asgard, waiting for the rising ocean of death to claim me?

She said, 'We can't stay here.'

'No,' Asgard agreed reluctantly. 'No, we can't.'

Hama, with Reth and Gemo, rode a platform of metal deep into the rocky heart of Callisto.

The walls of the pressurised shaft, sliding slowly upwards, were lined with slick transparent sheets, barring them from the ice. Hama reached out with a fingertip. The wall surface was cold and slippery, lubricated by a thin sheet of condensation from the chill air. There were no signs of structure, of strata in the ice; here and there small bores had been dug away from the shaft, perhaps as samples.

Callisto was a ball of dirty water ice. Save for surface impacts, nothing had happened to this moon since it accreted from the greater cloud that had formed the Jupiter system. The inner moons – Io, Europa, Ganymede – were heated, to one degree or another, by tidal pumping from Jupiter. So Europa, under a crust of ice, had a liquid ocean; and Io was driven by that perennial squeezing to spectacular volcanism. But Callisto had been born too far from her huge parent for any of that gravitational succour. Here, the only heat was a relic of primordial radioactivity; here there had been no geology, no volcanism, no hidden ocean.

Nevertheless, it seemed, Reth Cana had found life here. And, as the platform descended, Reth's cold excitement seemed to mount.

Nomi Ferrer was pursuing her own researches, in the settlement and out on the surface. But she had insisted that Hama be escorted by a squat, heavily-armed drone robot. Both Reth and Gemo ignored this silent companion, as if it were somehow impolite of Hama to have brought it along.

Nor did either of them mention Sarfi, who hadn't accompanied them. To Hama it did not seem human to disregard one's daughter, Virtual or otherwise. But then, what was *human* about a near-immortal traitor to the race? What was human about Reth, this man who had buried himself alone in the ice of Callisto, obsessively pursuing his obscure project, for decade after decade?

Even though the platform was small and cramped, Hama felt cold and alone; he suppressed a shiver.

The platform slowed, creaking, to a halt. He faced a chamber dug into the ice.

Reth said, 'You are a kilometre beneath the surface. Go ahead. Take a look.'

Hama saw that the seal between the lip of the circular platform and the roughly-cut ice was not perfect. He felt a renewed dread at his reliance on ancient, patched-up technology. But, suppressing hesitation, he stepped off the platform and into the ice chamber.

With a whir of aged bearings, the drone robot followed him.

Hama stood in a rough cube perhaps twice his height. It had been cut out of the ice, its walls lined by some clear glassy substance; it was illuminated by two hovering light globes. There was a knot of instrumentation, none of it familiar to Hama, along with a heap of data slates, some emergency equipment, and scattered packets of food and water. This was a working place, impersonal.

Reth stepped past him briskly. 'Never mind the gadgetry; you wouldn't understand it anyhow . . . *Look.*' And he snapped his fingers, summoning one of the floating globes. It came to hover at Hama's shoulder.

Hama leaned close to inspect the cut-away ice. He could see texture: the ice was a pale, dirty grey, polluted by what looked like fine dust grains – and, here and there, it was stained by colour, crimson and purple and brown.

Reth had become animated. 'I'd let you touch it,' he breathed. 'But the sheeting is there to protect *it* from *us* – not the other way around. The biota is much more ancient, unevolved, fragile than we are; the bugs on your breath might wipe it out in an instant. The prebiotic chemicals were probably delivered here by comet impacts during Callisto's formation. There is carbon and hydrogen and nitrogen and oxygen. The biochemistry is a matter of carbon-carbon chains and water – *like* Earth's, but not precisely so. Nothing *exactly* like our DNA structures . . .'

'Spell it out,' Gemo said casually, prowling around the gadgetry. 'Remember, Reth, the education of these young is woefully inadequate.'

'This is life,' Hama said carefully. 'Native to Callisto.'

'Life – yes,' Reth said. 'The highest forms are about equivalent to Earth's bacteria. But – native? I believe the life forms here have a common ancestor, buried deep in time, with Earth life – and with the more extravagant biota of Europa's buried ocean, and probably the living things found elsewhere in the Solar System. Do you know the notion of panspermia? Life, you see, may have originated in one place, perhaps even outside the System, and then was spread through the worlds by the spraying of meteorite-impact debris. And everywhere it landed, life embarked on a different evolutionary path.'

'But here,' Hama said slowly, fumbling to grasp these unfamiliar concepts, 'it was unable to rise higher than the level of a bacterium?'

'There is no room,' said Reth. 'There is liquid water here: just traces of it, soaked into the pores between the grains of rock and ice, kept from freezing by the radiogenic heat. But energy flows thin, and replication is very slow – spanning thousands of years.' He shrugged. 'Nevertheless there is a complete ecosystem . . . Do you understand? My Callisto bacteria are rather like the cryptoendoliths found in some inhospitable parts of the Earth. In Antarctica, for instance, you can crack open a rock and see layers of green life, leaching nutrients from the stone itself, sheltering from the wind and the desolating cold: communities of algae, cyanobacteria, fungi, yeasts –'

'Not any more,' Gemo murmured, running a finger over control panels. 'Reth, the Extirpation was *very* thorough, an effective extinction event; I doubt if any of your cryptoendoliths can still survive.'

'Ah,' said Reth. 'A pity.'

Hama straightened up, frowning. He had come far from the cramped caverns of the Conurbations; he was confronting life from another world, half a billion kilometres from Earth. He ought to feel wonder. But these pale shadows evoked only a kind of pity. Perhaps this thin, cold, purposeless existence was a suitable object for the obsessive study of a lonely, half-mad immortal.

Reth's eyes were on him, hard.

Hama said carefully, 'We know that before the Occupation the Solar System was extensively explored, by *Mykal Puhl* and those who followed him. The records of those times are lost – or hidden,' he said with a glance at the impassive Gemo. 'But we do know that everywhere the humans went, they found life. Life is commonplace. And in most places we reached, life has attained a much higher peak than *this*. Why not just catalogue these scrapings and abandon the station?'

Reth threw up his arms theatrically. 'I am wasting my

time. Gemo, how can this mayfly mind possibly grasp the subtleties here?'

She said dryly, 'I think it would serve you to try to explain, brother.' She was studying a gadget that looked like a handgun mounted on a floating platform. 'This, for example.'

When Hama approached this device, his weapon-laden drone whirred warningly. 'What is it?'

Reth stalked forward. 'It is an experimental mechanism based on laser light, which . . . It is a device for exploring the energy levels of an extended quantum structure.' He began to talk, rapidly, lacing his language with phrases like 'spectral lines' and 'electrostatic potential wells', none of which Hama understood.

At length Gemo interpreted for Hama.

'Imagine a very simple physical system – a hydrogen atom, for instance. I can raise its energy by bombarding it with laser light. But the atom is a quantum system; it can only assume energy levels at a series of specific steps. There are simple mathematical rules to describe the steps. This is called a "potential well".'

As he endured this lecture, irritation slowly built in Hama; it was clear there was much knowledge to be reclaimed from these patronising, arrogant pharaohs.

'The potential well of a hydrogen atom is simple,' said Reth rapidly. 'The simplest quantum system of all. It follows an inverse-square rule. But I have found the potential wells of much more complex structures –'

'Ah,' said Gemo. 'Structures embedded in the Callisto bacteria.'

'Yes.' Reth's eyes gleamed. He snatched a data slate from a pile at his feet. A series of numbers chattered over the slate, meaning little to Hama, a series of graphs that sloped sharply before dwindling to flatness: a portrait of the mysterious 'potential wells', perhaps.

Gemo seemed to understand immediately. 'Let me.' She took the slate, tapped its surface and quickly reconfigured the display. 'Now, look, Hama: the energies of the photons that are absorbed by the well are proportional to this series of numbers.'

1. 2. 3. 5. 7. 11. 13 . . .

'Prime numbers,' Hama said.

'Exactly,' snapped Reth. 'Do you see?'

Gemo put down the slate and walked to the ice wall; she ran her hand over the translucent cover, as if longing to touch the mystery that was embedded there. 'So inside each of these bacteria,' she said carefully, 'there is a quantum potential well that encodes prime numbers.'

'And much more,' said Reth. 'The primes were just the key, the first hint of a continent of structure I have barely begun to explore.' He paced back and forth, restless, animated. 'Life is never content simply to subsist, to cling on. Life seeks room to spread. That is another commonplace, young man. But here, on Callisto, there was no room: not in the physical world; the energy and nutrients were simply too sparse for that. And so –'

'Yes?'

'And so they grew *sideways*,' he said. 'And they reached orthogonal realms we never imagined existed.'

Hama stared at the thin purple scrapings and chattering

primes, here at the bottom of a pit with these two immortals, and feared he had descended into madness.

. . . 41. 43. 47. 53. 59 . . .

In a suit no more substantial than a thin layer of cloth, Nomi Ferrer walked over Callisto's raw surface, seeking evidence of crimes.

The sun was low on the horizon, evoking highlights from the curved ice plain all around her. From here, Jupiter was forever invisible, but Nomi saw two small discs, inner moons, following their endless dance of gravitational clockwork.

Gemo Cana had told her mayfly companions of how the Jovian system had once been. She told them of Io's mineral mines, nestling in the shadow of the huge volcano Babbar Patera. She told them of Ganymede: larger than Mercury, heavily cratered and geologically rich – the most stable and heavily populated of all the Jovian moons. And Europa's icy crust had sheltered an ocean hosting life, an ecosystem much more complex and rewarding than anybody had dreamed. 'They were *worlds*. Human worlds. All gone now, shut down by the Qax. But remember . . .'

Away from the sun's glare, lesser stars glittered, surrounding Nomi with immensity.

But it was a crowded sky, despite that immensity. Crowded and dangerous. For – she had been warned by the Coalition – the Xeelee craft that had glowered over Earth was now coming *here*, hotly pursued by a Spline ship retrieved from the hands of jasoft rebels and manned by Green Army officers. What would happen when that miniature armada got here, Nomi couldn't imagine.

The Xeelee were legends of a deep-buried, partly extirpated past. And perhaps they were monsters of the human future. The Xeelee were said to be godlike entities so aloof that humans might never understand their goals. Some scraps of Xeelee technology, like starbreaker beams, had fallen into the hands of 'lesser' species, like the Qax, and transformed their fortunes. The Xeelee seemed to care little for this – but, on occasion, they intervened.

To devastating effect.

Some believed that by such interventions the Xeelee were maintaining their monopoly on power, controlling an empire which, perhaps, held sway across the Galaxy. Others said that, like the vengeful gods of humanity's childhood, the Xeelee were protecting the 'junior races' from themselves.

Either way, Nomi thought, it's insulting. Claustrophobic. She felt an unexpected stab of resentment. We only just got rid of the Qax, she thought. And now this.

Gemo Cana had argued that in such a dangerous universe, humanity needed the pharaohs. 'Everything humans know about the Xeelee today, every bit of intelligence we have, was preserved by the pharaohs. I refuse to plead with you for my life. But I am concerned that you should understand. We pharaohs were not dynastic tyrants. We fought, in our way, to survive the Qax Occupation, and the Extirpation. For we are the wisdom and continuity of the race. Destroy us and you complete the work of the Qax for them, finish the Extirpation. Destroy us and you destroy your own past – which we preserved for you, at great cost to ourselves.'

Perhaps, Nomi thought. But in the end it was the bravery and ingenuity of one human – *a mayfly* – that had brought down the Qax, not the supine compromising of the jasofts and pharaohs.

She looked up towards the sun, towards invisible Earth. I just want a sky clear of alien ships, she thought. And to achieve that, perhaps we will have to sacrifice much.

Reth Cana began to describe where the Callisto bugs had 'gone'.

'There is no time,' he whispered. 'There is no space. This is the resolution of an ancient debate – do we live in a universe of perpetual change, or a universe where neither time nor motion exist? Now we understand. Now we know we live in a universe of static shapes. Nothing exists but the particles that make up the universe – that make up *us*. Do you see? And we can *measure* nothing but the separation between those particles.

'Imagine a universe consisting of a single elementary particle, an electron perhaps. Then there could be no space. For space is only the separation between particles. Time is only the measurement of changes in that separation. So there could be no time.

'Imagine now a universe consisting of *two* particles . . .'

Gemo nodded. 'Now you can have separation, and time.'

Reth bent and, with one finger, scattered a line of dark dust grains across the floor. 'Let each dust grain represent a distance – a configuration of my miniature two-particle cosmos. Each grain is labelled with a single number: the separation between the two particles.' He stabbed his finger into the line, picking out grains. '*Here* the particles are a metre apart; *here* a micron; *here* a light year. There is one special grain, of course: the one that represents zero separation, the particles overlaid. This diagram of dust shows all that is important about the underlying universe – the separation between its two components. And every possible configuration is shown at once, from this god-like perspective.'

He let his finger wander back and forth along the line, tracing out a twisting path in the grains. 'And here is a history: the two particles close and separate, close and separate. If they were conscious, the particles would think they were embedded in time, that they are coming near and far. But *we* can see that their universe is no more than dust grains, the lined-up configurations jostling against each other. It feels like time, inside. But from outside, it is just – sequence, a scattering of instants, of reality dust.'

Gemo said, 'Yes. "It is utterly beyond our power to measure the change of things by time. Quite the contrary, time is an abstraction at which we arrive by means of the changes of things."' She eyed Hama. 'An ancient philosopher. *Mach*, or *Mar-que* . . .'

'If the universe has three particles,' said Reth, 'you need *three* numbers. Three relative distances – the separation of the particles, one from the other – determine the cosmos's shape. And so the dust grains, mapping possible configurations, would fill up three-dimensional space – though there is still a unique grain, representing the special instant where all the particles are joined. And with four particles –'

'There would be six separation distances,' Hama said. 'And you would need a six-dimensional space to map the possible configurations.'

Reth glared at him, eyes hard. 'You are beginning to understand. Now. Imagine a space of stupendously many dimensions.' He held up a dust grain. 'Each grain represents one configuration of all the particles in *our* universe, frozen in time. This is reality dust, a dust of the Nows. And the dust fills *configuration space*, the realm of instants. Some of the dust grains may represent slices of our own history.' He snapped his fingers, once, twice, three times. 'There. There. There. Each moment, each juggling of the particles, a new grain, a new coordinate on the map. There is one grain that represents the coalescing of all the universe's particles into a single point. There are many more grains representing chaos – darkness – a random, structureless shuffling of the atoms.

'Configuration space contains all the arrangements of matter there could ever be. It is an image of eternity.' He waved a fingertip through the air. 'But if I trace out a path from point to point –'

'You are tracing out a history,' said Hama. 'A sequence of configurations, the universe evolving from point to point.'

'Yes. But *we* know that time is an illusion. In configuration space, all the moments that comprise our history
exist simultaneously. *And all the other configurations that
are logically possible also exist*, whether they lie along the
track of that history or not.'

Hama frowned. 'And the Callisto bugs –'

Reth smiled. 'I believe that, constrained in this space
and time, the Callisto lifeforms have started to explore
the wider realms of configuration space. Seeking a place
to play.'

Nomi turned away from the half-buried human town-
ship. She began to toil up the gentle slope of the ridge that
loomed above the settlement. This was one of the great
ring walls of the Valhalla system, curving away from this
place for thousands of kilometres, rising nearly a kilometre above the surrounding plains.

The land around her was silver and black, a midnight
sculpture of ridges and craters. There were no mountains here, none at all; any created by primordial
geology or the impacts since Callisto's birth had long
since subsided, slumping into formlessness. There was a
thin smearing of black dust over the dirty white of the
underlying ice; the dust was loose and fine-grained,
and she disturbed it as she passed, leaving bright footprints.

'Do you understand what you're looking at?'

The sudden voice startled her; she looked up.

It was Sarfi. She was dressed, as Nomi was, in a
translucent protective suit, another nod to the laws of

consistency that seemed to bind her Virtual existence. But she left no footprints, nor even cast a shadow.

Sarfi kicked at the black dust, not disturbing a single grain. 'The ice sublimes – did you know that? It shrivels away, a metre every ten million years – but it leaves the dust behind. That's why the human settlements were established on the north side of the Valhalla ridges. There it is just a shade colder, and some of the sublimed ice condenses out. So there is a layer of purer ice, right at the surface. The humans lived off ten-million-year frost . . . You're surprised I know so much. Nomi Ferrer, I was dead before you were born. Now I'm a ghost imprisoned in my mother's head. But I'm *conscious*. And I am still curious.'

Nothing in Nomi's life had prepared her for this conversation. 'Do you love your mother, Sarfi?'

Sarfi glared at her. 'She preserved me. She gave up part of herself for me. It was a great sacrifice.'

Nomi thought, You resent her. You resent this cloying, possessive love. And all this resentment bubbles inside you, seeking release. 'There was nothing else she could have done for you.'

'But I died anyway. I'm not *me*. I'm a download. I don't exist for me, but for *her*. I'm a walking, talking construct of her guilt.' She stalked away, climbing the slumped ice ridge.

Gemo started to argue detail with her brother. How was it possible for isolated bacteria-like creatures to form any kind of sophisticated sensorium? – but Reth believed there were slow pathways of chemical and electrical communication, etched into the ice and rock, tracks for great slow thoughts that pulsed through the substance of Callisto. Very well, but what of quantum mechanics? The universe was *not* made up of neat little particles, but was a mesh of quantum probability waves – ah, but Reth imagined quantum probability lying like a mist over his reality dust, constrained by two things: the geometry of configuration space, as acoustic echoes are determined by the geometry of a room; and something called a 'static universal wave function', a mist of probability that governed the likelihood of a given Now being experienced . . .

Hama closed his eyes, his mind whirling.

Blocky pixels flickered across his vision, *within* his closed eyes. Startled, he looked up.

Sarfi was kneeling before him; she had brushed her Virtual fingertips through his skull, his eyes. He hadn't even known she had come here.

'I know it's hard to accept,' she said. 'My mother spent a long time making me understand. You just have to open your mind.'

'I am no fool,' he said sharply. 'I can imagine a map of all the logical possibilities of a universe. But it would be just that – a map, a theoretical construct, a thing of data and logic. It would not be a *place*. The universe doesn't *feel* like that. I *feel* time passing. I don't experience disconnected instants, Reth's dusty reality.'

'Of course not,' said Reth. 'But you must understand that everything we know of the past is a record embedded in the present – the fossils and geology of Earth, so cruelly obliterated by the Qax, even the traces of chemicals and electricity in your own brain that comprise your memory, maintaining your illusion of past times . . . Gemo, may I –'

Gemo nodded, unsmiling.

Reth tapped a data slate. Sarfi froze, becoming a static, inanimate sculpture of light. Then, after perhaps ten seconds, she melted, began to move once more.

She saw Hama staring at her. 'What's wrong?'

Reth, ignoring her, said, 'The child contains a record of her own shallow past, embedded in her programs and data stores. She is unaware of intervals of time when she is frozen, or deactivated. If I could start and stop *you*, Hama Druz, you would wake protesting that your memories contained no gaps. But your memories themselves would have been frozen. I could even chop up your life and rearrange its instants in any way I chose; at each instant *you* would have an intact set of memories, a record of a past, and you would believe yourself to have lived through a continuous, consistent reality.

'And thus the maximal-reality dust grains contain *embedded within themselves* a record of the eras which "preceded" them. Each grain contains brains, like yours and mine, with "memories" embedded in them, frozen like sculptures. And history emerges in configuration space because those rich grains are then drawn, by a least-energy matching principle, to the grains which "precede" and "follow" them . . . You see?'

Sarfi looked to Gemo. 'Mother? What does he mean? . . .'

Gemo watched her clinically. 'Sarfi has been reset many times, of course,' she said absently. 'I had no wish to see her grow old, accreted with worthless memory. It was rather like the Extirpation, you see. The Qax sought to reset humanity, to abolish the memory of the race. In the ultimate realisation, we would have become a race of children, waking every day to a fresh world, every day a new creation. It was cruel, of course. But, theoretically, intriguing. Don't you think?'

Sarfi was trembling.

Now Reth began telling Gemo, rapidly and with enthusiasm, of his plans to explore his continent of configurations. 'No human mind could apprehend that multidimensional domain unaided, of course. But it can be modelled, with metaphors – rivers, seas, mountains. It is possible to *explore* it . . .'

Hama said, 'But, if your meta-universe is static, timeless, how could it be experienced? For experience depends on duration.'

Reth shook his head impatiently. He tapped his data slate and beckoned to Sarfi. 'Here, child.'

Hesitantly, she stepped forward.

She trailed a worm-like tube of light, as if her image had been captured at each moment in some invisible emulsion.

She emerged, blinking, at the other end of the tube, and looked back at it, bewildered.

'Stop these games,' Hama said tightly.

'You see?' Reth said. 'Here is an evolution of Sarfi's structure, but mapped in space, not time. But it makes no difference to Sarfi. Her memory at each frozen instant contains a record of her walking across the floor towards me – doesn't it, dear? And thus, in static configuration space, sentient creatures could have experiences, afforded them by the evolution of information structures across space.'

Hama turned to Sarfi. 'Are you all right?'

'What do you think?'

'I think Reth may be insane,' he said.

She stiffened, pulling back. 'Don't ask me. I'm not even a mayfly, remember?'

'It is a comforting philosophy, Hama,' Gemo said. 'Nothing matters, you see: not even death, not even the Extirpation. For we persist, each moment exists forever, in a great universe . . .'

It was a philosophy of decadence, Hama thought angrily. A philosophy of morbid contemplation, a consolation for ageless pharaohs as they sought to justify the way they administered the suffering of their fellow creatures. No wonder it appealed to them so much.

Gemo and Reth talked on, more and more rapidly, entering realms of speculation he couldn't begin to follow.

Callisto told Asgard what she was intending to do.

She walked along the narrowing beach, seeking scraps of people, of newborns and others, washed up by the pitiless black sea.

She picked up what looked like a human foot. It was oddly dry, cold, the flesh and even the bones crumbling at her touch.

She collected as many of these hideous shards as she could hold, and toiled back along the barren dust.

Then she worked her way through the forest back to the great tree, where she had encountered the creature called Night. She paused every few paces and pushed a section of corpse into the ground. She covered each fragment over with ripped-up grass and bits of bark.

'You're crazy,' Asgard said, trailing her, arms full of dried, crumbling flesh and bone.

'I know,' Callisto said. 'I'm going anyway.'

Asgard would not come far enough to reach the tree itself. So Callisto completed her journey alone.

Once more she reached the base of the tree. Once more, her heart thumping hard, she began to climb.

The creature, Night, seemed to have expected her. He moved from branch to branch, far above, a massive blur, and he clambered with ferocious purpose down the trunk.

She scrambled hurriedly back to the ground.

He followed her – but not all the way to the ground. He clung to his trunk, his broad face broken by that immense, bloody mouth, hissing at her.

She glowered back, and took a tentative step towards the tree. 'Come get me,' she muttered. 'What are you waiting for?' She took a piece of corpse (a *hand* – briefly her stomach turned), and she hurled it up at him.

He ducked aside, startled. But he swivelled that immense head. As the hand descended he caught it neatly in his scoop of a mouth, crunched once and swallowed it whole. He looked down at her with new interest.

And he took one tentative step towards the ground.

'That's it,' she crooned. 'Come on. Come eat the flesh. Come eat *me*, if that's what you want –'

Without warning he leapt from the trunk, immense hands splayed.

She screamed and staggered back. He crashed to the ground perhaps an arm's length from her. One massive fist slammed into her ankle, sending a stab of pain that made her cry out.

If he'd landed on top of her he would surely have crushed her.

The beast, winded, was already clambering to his feet.

She got to her feet and ran, ignoring the pain of her ankle. Night followed her, his lumbering four-legged pursuit slow but relentless. As she ran she kicked open her buried caches of body parts. He snapped them up and gobbled them down, barely slowing. The morsels seemed pathetically inadequate in the face of Night's giant reality.

She burst out onto the open beach, still running for her life. She reached the lip of the sea, skidding to a halt before the lapping black liquid. Her plan had been to reach the sea, to lure Night into it.

But when she turned, she saw that Night had hesitated on the fringe of the forest, blinking in the light. Perhaps he was aware that she had deliberately drawn him here.

He stepped forward deliberately, his immense feet sinking into the soft dust. There was no need for him to rush.

Callisto was already exhausted, and, trapped before the sea, there was nowhere for her to run.

Now he was out in the open she saw how far from the human form he had become, with his body a distorted slab of muscle, a mouth that had widened until it stretched around his head. And yet scraps of clothing clung to him, the remnants of a coverall of the same unidentifiable colour as her own. Once this creature, too, had been a newborn here, landing screaming on this desolate beach.

He towered over her, and she wondered how many unfortunates he had devoured to reach such proportions.

Beyond his looming shoulder, she could see Asgard, pacing back and forth along the beach.

'Great plan,' Asgard called. 'Now what?'

'I –'

Night raised up on his hind legs, huge hands pawing at the air over her head. He roared wordlessly, and bloody breath gushed over her.

Close your eyes, Callisto thought. This won't hurt.

'No,' Asgard said. She took a step towards the looming beast, began to run. 'No, no, *no*!' With a final yell she hurled herself at his back.

He looked around, startled, and swiped at Asgard with one giant paw. She was flung away like a scrap of bark, to land in a heap on the dust. But Night, off-balance, was stumbling backward, back toward the sea.

When his foot sank into the oily ocean, he looked down, as if surprised.

Even as he lifted his leg from the fluid the flesh was

drying, crumbling, the muscles and bone sloughing away in layers of purple and white. He roared his defiance, and cuffed at the sea – then gazed in horror at one immense hand left shredded by contact with the entropic ooze.

He began to fall, slowly, ponderously. Without a splash, the fluid opened up to accept his immense bulk. He was immediately submerged, the shallow fluid flowing eagerly over him.

In one last burst of defiance he broke the surface, mouth open, his flesh dissolving. His face was restored, briefly, to the human, his eyes a startling blue. He cried out, his voice thin: '*Reth!*'

The name sent a shiver of recognition through Callisto.

Then he fell back, and was gone.

She hurried to Asgard.

Asgard's chest was crushed, she saw immediately, imploded to an implausible degree, and her limbs were splayed around her at impossible angles. Her face was growing smooth, featureless, like a child's, beautiful in its innocence. Her gaze slid over Callisto.

Callisto cradled Asgard's head. 'This won't hurt,' she murmured. 'Close your eyes.'

Asgard sighed, and was still.

'Let me tell you about pharaohs,' Nomi said bitterly.

Hama listened in silence.

They stood on the Valhalla ridge, overlooking the old, dark settlement; the brightest point on the silver-black surface of Callisto was their own lifedome.

Nomi said, 'This was just after the Qax left. I got this

from a couple of our people who survived, who were *there*. There was a nest of the pharaohs, in one of the biggest Conurbations – one of the first to be constructed, one of the oldest. The pharaohs retreated into a pit, under the surface dwellings. They fought hard; we didn't know why. They had to be torched out. A lot of good people, good *mayflies*, died that day. When our people had dealt with the pharaohs, shut down the mines and drone robots and booby-traps . . . after all that, they went into the pit. It was dark. But it was warm, the air was moist, and there was movement everywhere. Small move-ments. And, so they say, there was a smell. Of *milk*.'

Nomi was silent for a long moment; Hama waited.

'Hama, I can't have children. I grew up knowing that. So maybe I ought to find some pity for the pharaohs. They don't breed true – like Gemo and Sarfi. But Sarfi is the exception, I think. Sometimes their children *are* born with Qax immortality. But –'

'Yes?'

'But they don't grow. They stop developing, at the age of two years or one year or six months or a month; some of them even stop growing before they are ready to be born, and have to be plucked from their mothers' wombs.

'And that was what our soldiers found in the pit, Hama. Racked up like specimens in a lab, hundreds of them. Must have been accumulating for centuries. Plugged into machines, mewling and crying.'

'Lethe.' Maybe Gemo is right, Hama thought; maybe the pharaohs really have paid a price we can't begin to understand.

'The pit was torched . . .'

Hama thought he saw a shadow pass across the sky, the scattered stars. 'Why are you telling me this, Nomi?'

Nomi pointed. 'There's a line of shallow graves over there. Not hard to find, in the end.'

'Ah.'

'The killings seemed to be uniform, the same method every time. A laser to the head. The bodies seemed peaceful,' Nomi mused. 'Almost as if they welcomed it.'

He had killed them. Reth had killed the other pharaohs who came here, one by one. But why?

And why would an immortal welcome death? Only if – his mind raced – only if she were promised a better place to go –

Everything happened at once.

A shadow, unmistakeable now, spread out over the stars: a hole in the sky, black as night, winged, purposeful. And, low towards the horizon, there was a flare of light.

'Lethe,' said Nomi softly. 'That was the GUTship. It's *gone* – just like that.'

'Then we aren't going home.' Hama felt numb; he seemed beyond shock.

'. . . Help me. Oh, help me . . .'

A form coalesced before them, a cloud of blocky pixels. Hama made out a sketch of limbs, a face, an open, pleading mouth. It was Sarfi, and she wasn't in a protective suit. Her face was twisted in pain; she must be breaking all her consistency overrides to have projected herself to the surface like this.

Hama held out his gloved hands, driven by an impulse to hold her; but that, of course, was impossible.

'Please,' she whispered, her voice a thin, badly-realised scratch. 'It is Reth. He plans to kill Gemo.'

Nomi set off down the ridge slope in a bouncing low-G run.

Hama said to Sarfi, 'Don't worry. We'll help your mother –'

Now he saw anger in that blurred, sketchy face. 'To Lethe with her! Save *me* . . .'

The pixels dispersed into a meaningless cloud, and winked out.

Callisto reached the great tree.

The trunk soared upwards, a pillar of rigid logic and history and consistency. She slapped its hide, its solidity giving her renewed confidence. And now there was no Night, no lurking monster, waiting up there to oppose her.

With purpose, ignoring the aches of her healing flesh and torn muscles, she began to climb.

As she rose above the trunk's lower tangle and encountered the merged and melded upper length, the search for crevices became more difficult, just as it had before. But she was immersed in the rhythm of the climb, and however high she rose there seemed to be pocks and ledges moulded into the smooth surface of the trunk, sufficient to support her progress.

Soon she had far surpassed the heights she had reached that first time she had tried. The mist was thick here, and when she looked down the ground was already lost: the great trunk rose from blank emptiness, as if rooted in nothingness.

But she thought she could see shadows, moving along the trunk's perspective-dwindled immensity: the others from the beach, some of them at least, were following her on her unlikely adventure.

And still she climbed.

The trunk began to split into great arcing branches that pushed through the thick mist. She paused, breathing deeply. Some of the branches were thin, spindly limbs that dwindled away from the main trunk. But others were much more substantial, great highways that seemed anchored to the invisible sky.

She picked the most solid-looking of these upper branches, and continued her climb.

Impeded by her damaged arm, her progress was slow but steady. It was actually more difficult to make her way along this tipped-over branch than it had been to climb the vertical trunk. But she was able to find handholds, and places where she could wrap her limbs around the branch.

The mist thickened further until she could see nothing around her but this branch: no sky or ground, not even the rest of this great tree, as if nothing existed but herself and the climb, as if the branch came from the mist and finished in the mist, a strange smooth surface over which she must toil forever.

And then, without warning, she broke through the mist.

*

In a pit dug into the heart of Callisto, illuminated by a single hovering globe lamp, Gemo Cana lay on a flat, hard pallet, unmoving.

Her brother stood hunched over her, working at her face with gleaming equipment. 'This won't hurt. Close your eyes . . .'

'Stop this!' Sarfi ran forward. She pushed her hands into Gemo's face, crying out as the pain of consistency violation pulsed through her.

Gemo turned, blindly. Hama saw that a silvery mask had been laid over her eyes, hugging the flesh there. 'Sarfi? . . .'

Nomi stepped forward, laser pistol poised. 'Stop this obscenity.'

Reth wore a mask of his own, a smaller cap that covered half his face; the exposed eye peered at them, hard, suspicious, calculating. 'Don't try to stop us. You'll kill her if you try. *Let us go*, Hama Druz.'

Nomi raised her pistol at his head.

But Hama touched the soldier's arm. 'Not yet.'

On her pallet, Gemo Cana turned her head blindly. She whispered, 'There's so much you don't understand.'

Hama snapped, 'You'd better make us understand, Reth Cana, before I let Nomi here off the leash.'

Reth paced back and forth. 'Yes – technically, this is a kind of death. But not a single one of the pharaohs who passed through here did it against his or her will.'

Hama frowned. ' "Passed through"?'

Reth stroked the metal clinging to Gemo's face; his sister turned her head in response. 'The core technology is an interface to the brain via the optic nerve. In this way I can connect the quantum structures which encode human consciousness to the structures stored in the Callisto bacteria – or rather, the structures which serve as, umm, a gateway to configuration space . . .'

Hama started to see it. 'You're attempting to download human minds into your configuration space.'

Reth smiled. 'It was not enough, you see, to study configuration space at second-hand, through quantum structures embedded in these silent bacteria. The next step had to be direct apprehension by the human sensorium.'

'The next step in what?'

'In our evolution, perhaps,' Reth murmured. 'With the help of the Qax, we have banished death. Now we can break down the walls of this shadow theatre we call reality.' He eyed Hama. 'This dismal pit is not a grave, but a gateway. And I am the gatekeeper.'

Hama said tightly, 'You destroy minds on the promise of afterlife – a promise concocted of theory and a scraping of cryptoendolith bacteria.'

'Not a theory,' Gemo whispered. 'I have *seen* it.'

Nomi grunted, 'We don't have time for this.'

But Hama asked, despite himself: 'What was it like?'

It was, Gemo said, a vast, spreading landscape, under a towering sky; she had glimpsed a beach, a rising, oily sea, an immense mountain shrouded in mist . . .

Reth stalked back and forth, arms spread wide. 'We remain human, Hama Druz. *I* cannot apprehend a multi-dimensional continuum. So I sought a metaphor. A

63
••

human interface. A beach of reality dust. A sea of – entropy, chaos. The structures folded into the living things, the shape of the landscape, represent consistency – what we time-bound creatures apprehend as causality.'

'And the rising sea –'

'The threat of the Xeelee,' he said, smiling thinly. 'The destruction to come. The obliteration of possibility. Even there, threats can reach . . . but life, mind can persist.

'Configuration space is real, Hama Druz. This isn't a new idea; *Pleh-toh* saw that, thousands of years ago . . . Ah, but you know nothing of *Pleh-toh*, do you? The higher manifold always existed, you see, long before the coming of mankind, of life itself. All that has changed is that through the patient, blind growth of the Callisto bacteria, I have found a way to reach it. And there, we can truly live forever –'

The ice floor shuddered, causing them to stagger.

Reth peered up the length of the shaft, smiling grimly. 'Ah. Our visitors make their presence known. Callisto is a small, hard, static world; it rings like a bell even at the fall of a footstep. And the footsteps of the Xeelee are heavy indeed . . .'

Sarfi pushed forward again, hands twisting, agonised by her inability to touch and be touched. She said to Gemo, 'Why do you have to *die*?'

Gemo's voice was slow, sleepy; Hama wondered what sedative agents Reth had fed her. 'You won't feel anything, Sarfi. It will be as if you never existed at all, as if all this pain never occurred. Won't that be better?'

The ground shuddered again, waves of energy from

some remote Xeelee-induced explosion pulsing through Callisto's patient ice, and the walls groaned, stressed.

Hama tried to imagine the black sea, the sharp-grained dust of the beach. Could it be true that Reth was accessing some meta-universe of theory and possibility – a place where every dust grain truly did represent an instant in *this* universe, a frozen slice of time, stars and galaxies and people and Xeelee and unfolding cosmos all embedded within?

But Hama had once visited the ocean – Earth's ocean – to oversee the reclamation of an abandoned Qax sea farm. He remembered the stink of ozone, the taste of salt in the damp air. He had hated it.

Reth seemed to sense his thoughts. 'Ah, but I forgot. You are creatures of the Conurbations, of the Extirpation. Of round-walled caverns and a landscape of grey dust. But this is how the Earth used to be, you see, before the Qax unleashed their nanotech plague. No wonder you find the idea strange. But not us.' He slipped his hand into his sister's. 'For us, you see, it will be like coming home.'

On the table, Gemo was convulsing, her mouth open, laced with drool.

Sarfi screamed, a thin wail that echoed from the high walls of the shaft. Once more she reached out to Gemo; once more her fluttering fingers passed through Gemo's face, sparkling.

'Gemo Cana is a collaborator,' Nomi said. 'Hama, you're letting her escape justice.'

Yes, Hama thought, surprised. Nomi, in her blunt way, had once more hit on the essence of the situation here. The pharaohs were the refugees now, and Reth's configuration space – if it existed at all – might prove their ultimate bolt-hole. Gemo Cana was escaping, leaving behind the consequences of her work, for good or ill.

But did that justify killing her?

The pharaoh turned her head.

Sarfi was crying. 'Mother, please. I'll die.'

'Hush,' said Gemo. 'You can't die. You were never alive. Don't you see that? You will always be with me, Sarfi. In a way. In my heart.' Her back arched. '*Oh . . .*'

Sarfi straightened and looked at her hands. The illusion of solidity was breaking down, Hama saw; pixels swarmed like fat, cubic insects, grudgingly cooperating to maintain the girl's form. Sarfi looked up at Hama with eyes like pits of darkness, and her voice was a flat, emotionless husk, devoid of intonation and character. '*Help me.*'

Again Hama reached out to her; again he dropped his hands, the most basic of human instincts invalidated. 'I'm sorry –'

'*It hurts.*' Her face swarmed with pixels that erupted and evaporated from the crumbling surface of her skin. Now the pixels fled her body, as if evaporating; she was becoming tenuous, unstable.

Hama forced himself to meet her gaze. 'It's all right,' he murmured. 'It will be over soon . . .' On and on, meaningless endearments; but she gazed into his eyes, as if seeking refuge there.

For a last instant her face congealed, clearly, from the

dispersing cloud. '*Oh . . .*' She reached up to him with a hand that was no more than a mass of diffuse light.

And then, with a silent implosion, her face crumbled, eyes closing.

Gemo shuddered once, and was still.

Hama could feel his heart pulse within him, the warm blood course. Nomi placed her strong hand on his shoulder, and he relished its fierce solidity.

Hama faced Reth. 'You are monsters.'

Reth smiled easily. 'Gemo is beyond your mayfly reproach. And as for the Virtual child – you may learn, Hama Druz, if you pass beyond your current limitations, that the first thing to be eroded by time is sentiment.'

Hama flared. 'I will never be like you, pharaoh. Sarfi was no toy.'

'But you still don't see it,' Reth said evenly. '*She is still alive* – but our time-bound language can't describe it – she persists, somewhere out there, beyond the walls of our petty realisation . . .'

Again the moon shuddered, and primordial ice groaned.

Reth murmured, 'Callisto was not designed to take such hammer blows . . . The situation is reduced, you see. *Now* there is only me.'

'And me.' Nomi raised the laser pistol.

'Is this what you want?' Reth asked of Hama. 'To cut down centuries of endeavour with a bolt of light?'

Hama shook his head. 'You really believe you can reach your configuration space – that you can survive there?'

'But I have proof,' Reth said. 'You saw it.'

'All I saw was a woman dying on a slab.'

Reth glowered at him. 'Hama Druz, make your decision.'

Nomi aimed the laser pistol.

'Let him go,' Hama said bitterly. 'He has only contempt for mayfly justice anyhow.'

Reth grinned and stepped back. 'You may be a mayfly, but you have the beginnings of wisdom, Hama Druz.'

'Yes,' Hama said quietly. 'Yes, I believe I do. Perhaps there *is* something there, some new realm of logic to be explored. But you, Reth, are blinded by your arrogance and your obsessions. Surely this new reality is nothing like the Earth of your childhood. And it will have little sympathy for your ambitions. Perhaps whatever survives the download will have no resemblance to *you*. Perhaps you won't even remember who you were. What then?'

Reth's mask sparkled; he raised his hand to his face. He made for the pallet, to lie beside the cooling body of his sister. But he stumbled and fell before he got there.

Hama and Nomi watched, neither moving to help him.

Reth, on his hands and knees, turned his masked face to Hama. 'You can come with me, Hama Druz. To a better place, a higher place.'

'You go alone, pharaoh.'

Reth forced a laugh. Then he cried out, his back arching.

He fell forward, and was still.

Nomi raked the body with laser fire. 'Good riddance,' she growled. '*Now* can we get out of here?'

*

There was a mountain.

It rose high above the night-dark sea, proudly challenging the featureless, glowing sky. Rivers flowed from that single great peak, she saw: black and massive, striping its huge conical flanks, merging into great tumbling cascades that poured into the ocean.

The mountain was the centre of the world, thrusting from the sea.

She was high above an island, a small scrap of land that defied the dissolving drenching of the featureless sea. Islands were few, small, scattered, threatened everywhere by the black, crowding ocean.

But, not far away, there was another island, she saw, pushing above the sea of mist. It was a heaping of dust on which trees grew thickly, their branches tangled. In fact the branches reached across the neck of sea that separated this island from her own. She thought she could see a way to reach that island, scrambling from tree to tree, following a great highway of branches.

The other island rose higher than her own above the encroaching sea. There, she thought, she – and whoever followed her – would be safe from lapping dissolution. For now, anyhow.

But what did that mean? What would Pharaoh have said of this – that the new island was an unlikely heap of reality dust, further from looming entropic destruction?

She shook her head. The deeper meaning of her journey scarcely mattered – and nor did its connection to any other place. If this world were a symbol, so be it:

this was where she lived, and this was where she would, with determination and perseverance, survive.

She looked one last time at the towering mountain. Damaged arm or not, she itched to climb it, to challenge its negentropic heights. But in the future, perhaps. Not now.

Carefully, clinging to her branch with arms and legs and her one good hand, she made her way along the branch to the low-probability island. One by one, the people of the beach followed her.

In the mist, far below, she glimpsed slow, ponderous movement: huge beasts, perhaps giant depraved cousins of Night. But, though they bellowed up at her, they could not reach her.

Once more Hama and Nomi stood on the silver-black surface of Callisto, under a sky littered with stars. Just as before, the low, slumped ridges of Valhalla still marched to the silent horizon.

But this was no longer a world of antiquity and stillness. The shudders were coming every few minutes now. In places the ice crust was collapsing, ancient features subsiding, here and there sending up sprays of dust and ice splinters that sparkled briefly before falling back, all in utter silence.

Hama thought back to a time before this assignment, to the convocations he had joined. He had been a foolish boy, he thought, his ideas half-formed. Now, when he looked into his heart, he saw crystal-hard determination.

'No more pharaohs,' Hama murmured. 'No more

immortality. That way lies arrogance and compromise and introversion and surrender. A brief life burns brightly.'

Nomi growled, 'More theory, Hama? Let's count the ways we might die. The Xeelee starbreaker might cream us. One of these miniature quakes might erupt right under us. Or maybe we'll last long enough to suffocate in our own farts, stuck inside these damn suits. What do you think? I don't know why you let that arrogant pharaoh kill himself.'

Hama murmured, 'You see death as an escape?'

'If it's easy, if it's under your control – yes.'

'Reth did escape,' Hama said. 'But I don't think it was into death.'

'You *believed* all that stuff about theoretical worlds?'

'Yes,' Hama said. 'Yes, in the end I think I did believe it.'

'Why?'

'Because of *them*.' He gestured at the sky. 'The Xeelee. If our second-hand wisdom has any validity at all, we know that the Xeelee react to *what they fear*. And almost as soon as Reth constructed his interface to his world of logic and data, as soon as the pharaohs began to pass into it, they came here.'

'You think the Xeelee fear us?'

'Not us. The bugs in the ice: Reth's cryptoendoliths, dreaming their billion-year dreams . . . The Xeelee seem intent on keeping those dreams from escaping. And that's why I think Reth hit on a truth, you see. Because the Xeelee see it too.'

Now, over one horizon, there was a glowing crimson cloud, like dawn approaching – but there could be no dawn on this all-but-airless world.

'Starbreaker light,' murmured Nomi. 'The glow must be vapour, ice splinters, dust, thrown up from the trench they are digging.'

Hama felt a fierce anger burn. 'Once again aliens have walked into our System, for their own purposes, and we can do nothing to stop them. This mustn't happen again, Nomi. Let this be an end – and a beginning, a new Day Zero. You know, perhaps the Qax were right to attempt the Extirpation. If we are to survive in this dangerous universe we must remake ourselves, without sentiment, without nostalgia, without pity. History is irrelevant. Only the future is important.' He longed to be gone from this place, to bring his hard new ideas to the great debates that were shaping the future of mankind.

'You're starting to frighten me, my friend,' Nomi said gently. 'But not as much as *that*.'

Now the Xeelee nightfighter itself came climbing above the shattered fog of the horizon. It was like an immense, black-winged bird. Hama could see crimson starbreaker light stab down into the passive, defenceless ice of Callisto. The shuddering of the ground was constant now, as that mass of shattered ice and steam rolled relentlessly towards them.

Nomi grabbed onto him; holding each other, they struggled to stay on their feet as ice particles battered their faceplates. A tide of destruction spanned Callisto from horizon to horizon. There was, of course, no escape.

And then the world turned silver, and the stars swam.

Hama cried out, clinging to Nomi, and they fell. They hit the ice hard, despite the low gravity.

Nomi, combat-hardened, was on her feet immediately. An oddly pink light caught her squat outline. But Hama, winded, bewildered, found himself gazing up at the stars.

Different stars? No. Just – moved. The Xeelee ship was gone, vanished.

He struggled to his feet.

The wave of vapour and ice was subsiding, as quickly as it had been created; there was no air here to prevent the parabolic fall of the crystals back to the shattered land, little gravity to prevent the escape of the vapour into Jovian space. The land's shuddering ceased, though he could feel deep slow echoes of huge convulsions washing through the rigid ground . . .

But the stars had moved.

He turned, taking in the changed sky. Surely the shrunken sun was a little further up the dome of sky. And a pink slice of Jupiter now showed above the smoothly curved horizon, where none had shown before on this tide-locked moon.

Nomi touched his arm, and pointed deep into the ice. '*Look.*'

It was like some immense fish, embedded in the ground, its spread-eagled black wings clearly visible through layers of dusty ice. A red glow shone fitfully at its heart; as Hama watched it sputtered, died, and the buried ship grew dark.

Nomi said, 'At first I thought the Xeelee must have lit up some exotic super-drive and got out of here. But I was wrong. That thing must be half a kilometre down. How did it *get* there?'

'I don't think it did,' Hama said. He turned away and peered at Jupiter. '*I think Callisto moved*, Nomi.'

'What . . . ?'

'It didn't have to be far. Just a couple of kilometres. Just enough to swallow up the Xeelee craft.'

Nomi was staring at him. 'That's insane, Hama, what can move a moon?'

Why, a child could, Hama thought in awe. A child playing on a beach – if every grain on that beach is a slice in time.

I see a line sketched in the dust, a history, smooth and complete. I pick out a grain with Callisto positioned just *here*. And I replace it with a grain in which Callisto is positioned just a little further over *there*. As easy, as wilful, as that.

No wonder the Xeelee are afraid.

A new shuddering began, deep and powerful.

'Lethe,' said Nomi. 'What now?'

Hama shouted, 'Not the Xeelee this time. Callisto spent four billion years settling into its slow waltz around Jupiter. Now I think it's going to have to learn those lessons over again.'

'Tides,' Nomi growled.

'It might be enough to melt the surface. Perhaps those cryptoendoliths will be wiped out after all. I wonder if the Xeelee *planned* it that way all along . . .'

He saw a slow grin spread across Nomi's face. 'We aren't done yet.' She pointed.

Hama turned. A new moon was rising over Callisto's tight horizon. It was a moon of flesh and metal, and it bore a sigil, a blue-green tetrahedron, burned into its hide.

'The Spline ship, by Lethe,' Nomi said. She punched Hama's arm. 'So the story goes on, my friend.'

Hama glared down into the ice, at the Xeelee craft buried there. Yes, the story goes on. But we have introduced a virus into the software of the universe. And I wonder what eyes will be here to see, when that ship is finally freed from this tortured ice.

An orifice opened up in the Spline's immense hide. A flitter squirted out and soared over Callisto's ice, seeking a place to land.

Exhausted, disoriented, Callisto and her followers stumbled down the last length of trunk and collapsed to the ground.

She dug her good hand into the loose grains of reality dust. She felt a surge of pride, of achievement. This island, an island of a new possibility, was her island now.

Hers, perhaps, but not empty, she realised slowly. There was a newborn here: lost, bewildered, suddenly arrived. She saw his face smoothing over, working with anguish and doubt, as he *forgot*.

But when his gaze lit on her, he became animated.

He tried to stand, to walk towards her. He stumbled, weak and drained, and fell on his face.

Dredging up the last of her own strength, she went to him. She dug her hand under him and turned him on his back – as, once, Pharaoh had done for her.

He opened his mouth. Spittle looped between his lips, and his voice was a harsh rasp. 'Gemo!' he gasped. 'I made you! Help me! Love me!'

Something tugged at her: recognition – and resentment.

She held his head to her chest. 'This won't hurt,' she said. 'Close your eyes.' And she held him, until the last of his unwelcome memories had leaked away, and, forgetting who he was, he lay still.

'I find it surprisingly difficult to articulate why I so intensely admire Paul McAuley's work. Perhaps the problem is simply that it is so uniformly excellent. Once I say that I admire his fine, clean, prose, the clarity of his plotting, the originality of his ideas, his understanding of science, and the quality of his characterisation, what else is there to say? To list his good qualities is the same as to list those things I like about science fiction.' *Michael Swanwick*

PAUL McAULEY
Making History

Copyright © Paul McAuley 2000

The right of Paul McAuley to be identified as the author
of this work has been asserted in accordance with the
Copyright, Designs and Patents Act of 1988.

This edition published in Great Britain in 2002 by

Gollancz
An imprint of the Orion Publishing Group
Orion House, 5 Upper St Martin's Lane,
London, WC2H 9EA

A CIP catalogue record for this book
is available from the British Library.

ISBN 0 575 07306 3

Typeset at The Spartan Press Ltd,
Lymington, Hants

Printed in Great Britain by
Clays Ltd, St Ives plc

I believe that I first saw Demi Lacombe at the gala reopening of the theatre. She had arrived in Paris, Dione a week before, but I am sure that, had I passed her in one of the gardens or arcades of the diplomatic quarter, or glimpsed her at one of the receptions or *soirées* or cocktail parties or conversations, I would have remembered her, for in an age where beauty could be cheaply bought, hers was a rare and natural wonder, and not easily forgotten.

So I am certain that we first met that night, at the touring company production of *Don Giovanni*. The theatre of Paris, Dione, was one of the first buildings in the city's main dome to have been restored after the end of the siege. Although the gala performance that marked its reopening was an overt symbol of the occupation force's power, it was the first time many of the force's executives and officials had ventured outside the diplomatic quarter. It was preceded by speeches made more to the media (represented by a single journalist and a dozen remotes) than to the audience, for it was the kind of event that politicians fondly believe will enhance their status, but which usually wins not so much as a footnote in the pages of history.

The theatre was a roofless bowl modelled in miniature on Rome's ruined Colosseum. Tiers of seats and private boxes rose steeply all around the circular stage to the rim, where armoured troopers and angular killing machines patrolled, tiny shadows against the artificial night. The colonists, who had fought to the death for freedom from Earth's rule, had kept to the twenty-four hour diurnal cycle of their home planet; the panes of the dome, high above, were polarised against the wan light of Dione's midday, and the suspensor lamps were turned down to mere stars.

On the stage's glowing dish, the cast flitted and swarmed through a web of wires and stays like a flock of gaudy birds, freezing in emblematic tableaux during the great arias. The lacklustre production had been foolishly gussied up in modern dress, with the Commendatore a robot, Don Giovanni a dispossessed captain of a Kuiper Belt habitat driven mad by a bioweapon symbiont, his servant Leporello an ambitious neuter who borrowed something of Iago's malevolent glee at the ordinary human weaknesses of its extraordinary master. From the vantage of my fifth tier box, I paid as much attention to the audience as I did to the familiar allegory of the priapic Don's damnation, and two people in a box on the same level as mine quickly caught my eye. One was someone I had come to know well, Cris DeHon, head of the team that was reconstructing the city's information network; DeHon's companion was as breathtaking as she was incongruous. After the statue of the Commendatore had sprung to life and consigned the Don to his doom amidst flares of flame and writhing, red-skinned demons,

after the ritual of applause and encore, DeHon found me at the post-performance party which, in truth, was more important to most of the audience than the opera's choreographed histrionics.

'Dr Lacombe has an interest in history,' DeHon told me, after it had made the introductions. Like Leporello, the Don's servant, Cris DeHon was a neuter, one of the few people in the room who could not be affected, except in a purely aesthetic sense, by Dr Lacombe's beauty. And like Leporello, it was consumed by a feverish delight in fomenting intrigue. Perhaps intrigue was to it as sex was to most men and women. It was a brilliant and vicious gossip, and a generous source of unreliable information.

'Indeed,' I said, helplessly, foolishly smiling at DeHon's companion. I confess that, like most men in the chamber, and not a few women, I could not take my eyes from her. She was so unspeakably lovely, swaying gracefully in the low gravity about the anchor point of her sticky shoes like a nereid on some sea's floor. When I dared to lift her gloved right hand by the tips of her fingers, and bent over her knuckles, the gorgeous creature actually blushed. She was young, and seemed to have not yet grown into her beauty, for she wore it as carelessly as a child costumed in some fabulously antique robe, and was simultaneously embarrassed and amused by the reactions she provoked. Perhaps even then she had a presentiment that it would be the cause of her death.

She said, so softly I had to lean close to hear her, 'I am no more than an amateur of history. But of course I have heard of your work, Professor-Doctor Graves.'

Her Portuguese had a soft, husky lilt. A subtle perfume, with a deep note of musk, rose from the cleft between her breasts, which were displayed to their advantage by the blood-red folds of her spidersilk blouson. A wide belt of red leather measured the narrowness of her waist; red silk trousers, cuffed at the ankles, gathered in complex pleats around her long, slim legs. Her hair was silver and frost; her eyes beaten copper flecked with green.

'Demi is too modest,' DeHon said. 'Her monograph on the conceptual failures in design of early orbital habitats is something of a classic.'

I noted that the ghost of a double chin appeared when Demi Lacombe dipped her head in quiet acknowledgement of DeHon's compliment, and that her bare arms were plump and rosy. I thought then that if she ever had children the natural way, she would have to take care not to grow fat, and it was a relief to realise that her beauty was only mortal.

She said, 'Cris is probably the only one, apart from myself and my thesis supervisor, who has read all of it.'

'I like to keep up with our cultural guests,' DeHon said.

'I'm really more of an engineer,' Demi Lacombe told me. 'What they did here, with the city parklands, that was true artistry.'

I learnt that she was an environmental engineer, brought to Dione by the Three Powers Occupation Force to survey Paris's damaged ecosystem and to suggest how it could be reconstructed.

When I expressed interest, she deflected it automatically. 'I am not here to do anything radical. Just to figure

out the best way to make the city habitable again. But for a historian to find himself right at the centre of history in the making must be tremendously exciting.'

'The war is over. This gala performance was deliberately staged to make the point. I'm merely picking over its ruins.'

'Is it true that you go out into the city without any guards?'

'I have a guide. I need to talk to people when they are at their ease. Bringing them to the diplomatic quarter has unfortunate implications.'

'Arrest,' DeHon said, with a delicate, refined shudder. 'Interrogation.'

I said, 'I do carry a weapon, but it's as unnecessary as the guards who patrol the perimeter of the theatre. The survivors of the siege are by now quite inured to their fate. It's true that many areas of the city are still dangerous, but only because of unrepaired damage and a few undiscovered booby traps.'

'Do you believe,' Demi Lacombe asked, boldness making her eyes shine, 'that he still lives?'

I knew at once who she meant, of course, as would anyone in Paris. I said, 'Of course not.'

'Yet I'm told that many of the survivors think that he does.'

'It is a frail and foolish hope, but hope is all they have. No, he willed his death from the beginning, when he assassinated the rest of the emergency committee and despoiled the diplomatic quarter, and he sealed his fate when he killed his hostages and the diplomats sent to

5
.

bargain for peace. He was not the kind of man to run away from the consequences of his actions and so, like most of those he briefly commanded, he would have been killed in the siege. His body has not yet been identified, but the same can be said for more than half of those killed.'

'You are very certain.'

'I have studied human nature all my life.'

'And would you classify him as one of your great men?'

'I'm flattered that you know of my work.'

Demi Lacombe said, 'I wouldn't lie for the sake of politeness, Professor-Doctor Graves.'

'Please, Mademoiselle, I think we might be friends. And my friends call me Fredo.'

'And so shall I, because I don't really get on with this false formality. I know it's the fashion in the Pacific Community, but I'm a hick from Europe. So, Fredo, is he a great man?'

The delicate suffusion of her soft cheeks: alabaster in the first light of morning.

I bowed and said, 'The corporados think so, or they would not have sponsored my research. However, I have not yet made up my mind.'

As we talked, I was aware of the people, mostly men, who were watching Demi Lacombe from near and far. The architects of the cities of the moons of the outer planets, imaginations stimulated by the engineering possibilities of microgravity, made their public spaces as large as possible, to relieve the claustrophobia of their tents and domes and burrows. The theatre's auditorium, a great crescent wedged beneath the steep slope of the

seats, could easily have held two thousand people, and although almost everyone in the diplomatic quarter had come to the gala opening, we numbered no more than three hundred, scattered sparsely across the vast, black floor, which our shoes gripped tightly in lieu of proper gravity. Diplomats, executives and officials of the *ad hoc* government; *novo abastado* industrialists, sleek as well-fed sharks, trailed by entourages of aides and bodyguards as they lazily cruised the room, hoping to snap up trifles and titbits of gossip; officers of the Three Powers Occupation Force, in the full dress uniforms of half a dozen different armies; collaborationists in their best formal wear, albeit slightly shabby and out of fashion, mostly *en famille* and mostly gorging themselves at the buffet, for rationing was still in force amongst Paris's defeated population.

There was a stir as, in full costume and make-up, Don Giovanni and Leporello escorted Donna Anna and Donna Elvira into the huge room. The actors half-swam, half-walked through the web of tethers with consummate ease, acknowledging the scattering of applause. At the centre of the auditorium's crescent, one man, sleek, dark-haired, in an immaculate pearly uniform, had not turned to watch the actors but was still staring openly at Demi Lacombe. It was Dev Veeder, the dashing colonel in charge of the security force. When Demi Lacombe looked up and saw him watching her I thought I heard the snap of electricity between them.

DeHon nudged me and said loudly, for the benefit of everyone nearby, 'Our brave colonel is smitten, don't you think?'

I should not have allowed myself to become involved, of course. But like Cris DeHon (although I was neutered by age and temperament rather than by elective treatment), I had a bystander's fascination with human sexual behaviour. And, frankly, my assignment, although lucratively paid, was becoming tiresome.

I had been in Paris, Dione for two months, commissioned by a consortium of half a dozen Greater Brazilian corporados to write an official history of the siege of the city, and in particular to contribute to a psychological model of Marisa Bassi, the leader of the barricades, the amateur soldier who had kept off the forces of the Three Powers Alliance for twenty days after the general surrender which had brought an end of the Quiet War elsewhere in the solar system.

I knew that I had been chosen because of my position as emeritus professor of history at Rio de Janeiro rather than for my ability or even my reputation, tattered as it was by the sniping of jealous younger colleagues. Historians cannot reach an agreement about anything, and most especially they cannot agree on the way history is

made. Herodotus and Thucydides believed that the proper subjects of history were war and constitutional history and political personality, times of crisis and change; Plutarch suggested that history was driven by the actions and desires of exemplary characters, of great men. The Christians introduced God into history, a kind of alpha great man presiding over a forced marriage of divine and human realms, and when the notion of an epicurean God was shouldered aside in the Renaissance, the idea that history was shaped by forces beyond the control of ordinary men remained, although these forces were no longer centred on extraordinary individuals but were often considered to be no more than blind chance, the fall of a coin, the want of a nail. Like a maggot in an apple, chance lay at the heart of Gibbon's elegant synthesis of the philosophical studies of Voltaire and the systematic organisation of facts by rationalists like Hume and Montesquieu; it was the malignant flaw in Leopold von Ranke's (a distant ancestor of mine) codification of history as a neutral, non-partisan, scholarly pursuit; and it was made explicit in the twentieth century fragmentation of the history of ideas into a myriad specialities and the levelling of all facts to a common field, so that the frequency of dental caries in soldiers in the trenches of the First World War was considered as important an influence of events as the abilities of generals. Great men or small, all were tossed alike by society's tides.

It was not until the restoration of history as a species of literature, by deployment of virtual theatre and

probabilistic clades, that the idea of the worth of the individual was restored. Who can say if this view of history caused the collapse of democratic republicanism, or if republicanism's collapse changed our philosophy of history? But it is certain that the rise of nationalism and the restoration of half-forgotten monarchies, aided by supranational corporados which found it convenient to divide their commercial territories into quarrelling kingdoms and principalities, paralleled the return of the theory of the great man in history, a theory of which I, in my time, was an important champion.

In my time.

I had hoped that by coming to Paris, Dione, in the midst of reconstruction of a war scarcely ended, I would be able to secure my reputation with a final masterwork and confound my jealous rivals. But I soon discovered that the last days of the free collective of Paris, and of its leader, Marisa Bassi, were a tissue of echoes and conflicting stories supported by too few solid facts.

Those few surviving collectivists who believed that Marisa Bassi was dead could not agree how or where he had died; the majority, who foolishly believed that he had escaped during the hours of madness when special forces of the Three Powers Alliance had finally infiltrated the city, could not agree on how he had escaped, nor where he had escaped to. No ship had left Dione in those last desperate days except the cargo scow that, its navigation system driven mad by viral infection, had ploughed into Saturn's thick atmosphere and had either burned up or now floated, squashed to a two-dimensional profile by

crushing atmospheric pressure, near the planet's metallic hydrogen core.

If history is a story told by winners, then the winners have the unconscionable burden of sifting mountains of dross for rare nuggets of pure fact, while the losers are free to fantasise on what could or should have been.

My commission should have been simple, but I found the demands of my employers, who did not trouble to supply me with assistants, were stretching my methodology to its breaking point. The corporados wanted to capture the psyche of a great rebel leader in a heuristic model, a laboratory specimen of a troublesome personality they could study and measure and define, as doctors begin to fight a disease by first unravelling the genetic code of the virus, bacterium or faulty gene that is its cause. By knowing what Marisa Bassi had been, they thought that they could prevent another of his kind gaining power in the half-ruined colonies.

After two months, I had a scant handful of facts about Marisa Bassi's life before the Quiet War, and a horrible knot of evasions and half-truths and lies about his role in the siege, a knot that became more complex each day, with no way of cutting through to the truth. I confess, then, that in the days following my first meeting with Demi Lacombe, I was more interested in the rumours and gossip about her and Dev Veeder than in my own work.

It was, you must understand, an interest born of concern for her safety: an almost paternal concern. There was our age difference – almost fifty years – and my devotion to the memory of my dear dead wife. No matter what

others may say, I had only pure motives in taking an interest in Dev Veeder's assault on the heart of the young and beautiful environmental engineer.

At first, much of my information came from Cris DeHon, who told me how our head of security personally escorted Demi Lacombe as she surveyed and catalogued the ruined wildernesses and parklands and farms of the city, assiduously transporting her to wherever she desired, arranging picnics in a sealed house or in a bubble habitat laboriously swept clear of booby traps and biowar beasties by squads of troopers. And like everyone else in the claustrophobic shark-pool of Paris's diplomatic quarter, I saw how closely Dev Veeder attended Demi Lacombe at every social gathering, even though she spent most of her time with the science crews while he stood by impotently, unable to participate in their impenetrable, jargon-ridden conversations.

'It's a purely one-sided affair,' DeHon told me, when it caught me watching her at a party held by one or another of the corporados, I forget which, on the huge lawn at the centre of the diplomatic quarter, part of the parkland that both penetrated and surrounded the built-up area inside the quarter's pyramidal tent. As always, most of us were there, scattered across an oval of brilliant green grass webbed with tethers, the dozens of faint shadows overlapping at our feet cast by brilliant lamps hung from the high ridge of the quarter's roof, Saturn's foggy crescent tilted beyond like a fantastic brooch pinned to a sky as black as jeweller's velvet. In the shade of the efflorescent greenery of a sweet chestnut tree, that sprawled like a

banyan in the low gravity, Demi Lacombe was talking earnestly with a couple of techheads; Dev Veeder stood close by in his dress uniform, watching her over the rim of the wine bulb from which, every now and then, he pretended to sip.

Cris DeHon said, 'She's such an innocent: she really doesn't see how badly she is humiliating Dev. You've heard how he's increased the number of security sweeps in the general population? I do believe that it is a reliable index of his growing frustration. I think that soon there will be more public executions, unknowing sacrifices on the altar of our gallant police chief's unrequited love.'

I said, perhaps a trifle sharply, 'What do you know of love?'

'Love or lust,' the neuter said, 'it's all the same. Love is merely the way by which men fool themselves that they have nobler motives than merely spending their urges, a game sprung from the constant tension between the male's blind need to copulate and the female's desire to win a father who will help provide for her children. Our security chief is parading like a peacock because he knows he is competing against every potential suitor of the delicious Mademoiselle Lacombe. And how many suitors there are!' DeHon bent closer and whispered, 'I hear she takes long night walks in the parkland.'

Its breath smelt of milk and cinnamon: a baby's breath.

'That's hardly surprising,' I said. 'She is an environmental engineer. The gardens must fascinate her.'

'I've heard she has a particular interest in the gardeners.'

I laughed. 'That would be obscene if it were not so ridiculous.'

Cris DeHon's smile showed small pearl-white teeth. 'Perhaps. But perhaps poor beautiful Demi seeks simple relief from the strain of being the focus of a killer's desire.'

I suppose the epithet was not an exaggeration, although it shocked me then, as no doubt DeHon hoped it would. Dev Veeder had had a good war, and had risen quickly through the ranks of the Greater Brazilian Army. He was a war hero, although like many heroes of the Quiet War – at least, on the winning side – he had never engaged in combat. His speciality was debriefing; I suppose a more liberal age might say that he was a torturer, although his methods were as much psychological as physical. He once confided to me that showing a prisoner the instruments he proposed to use often had as much effect as application of the instruments themselves – especially if the prisoner had been forced to listen to the screams of others suffering hot questioning. Early in the war, Dev Veeder had interrogated an entire mining community on Europa, some fifty men, women and children; the intelligence he had wrung from them had helped bring a swift and relatively bloodless end to the siege of Minos. This and other exploits had won him his present position of head of security of Paris, which he prosecuted with diligence and vigour.

Dev Veeder was young, the youngest son of a good family with connections in both industry and government. He was fiercely ambitious and highly intelligent. He had a sharp black impatient gaze. His hair was combed

back in waves from his high forehead and aquiline nose; his make-up was discreetly but skilfully applied. A dandy from the pages of a seventeenth century novel, but no fool. I knew him well from the conversations we had had about history. He was very interested in my theories, and believed, like many middle-ranking military men, that he himself had something of the attributes of a great man. This vanity was his single serious weakness, although it was true that, like all tyrants, he believed himself both benevolent and pragmatic.

'If only I had had the chance to really prove myself,' he said to me more than once, showing that he really misunderstood my theory. For great men of history do prove themselves; the will to succeed, not luck or circumstance, is what makes them great. They rise to the occasion; they seize the day; they mould themselves to be all things to all men. Dev Veeder was too proud to realise this, and perhaps too cruel. He could only be what he was, and perhaps that is why I feared for Demi, and why I crossed him.

Three

Each day, I left the safety of the diplomatic quarter for the ruins of the city to interview the survivors of the siege, to try and learn what they knew or claimed to know about Marisa Bassi. In spite of my reputation and the letters of commission I carried, Dev Veeder did not think that I was important enough to warrant a proper escort – an impertinence for which I was grateful, for one cannot properly conduct interviews amongst a defeated population in the presence of troopers of the force that now occupies their territory. And so, each day, armed only with the blazer that I kept holstered at my ankle, I set out to pursue my research in the refugee warrens.

It was my custom to wait for my guide in a small café at the edge of the small plaza just outside the diplomatic quarter. The place had once been the checkpoint for the quarter, with cylinder gates to control access and human guards on duty in case there was a problem the computer was not authorised to handle. On the night of the revolution, a mob had stormed the guardhouse and killed the guards, fried the computer and associated security hard-

ware with an industrial microwave beam, and blown the gates. The diplomatic quarter had already been evacuated, but a small detachment of soldiers and minor executives had been left behind as caretakers; no one had expected the revolutionary committee to violate the diplomatic quarter's sovereign status. The soldiers killed half a hundred of the mob before they were themselves killed, the surviving executives were taken hostage, and the buildings looted.

After the war, the quarter was the first place to be restored, of course, and a memorial had been erected to the murdered soldiers and martyred hostages, virtually the only casualties on our side. But the ruins of the gates still stood to one side of the plaza on which half a dozen pedways and escalators converged, tall hollow columns gutted of their armatures, their bronze facings scorched and ghosted with half-erased slogans.

The guardhouse's airy teepee was slashed and half-collapsed, but an old married couple had set up a tiny kitchen inside it and put a scattering of mismatched chairs and tables outside. Perhaps they hoped to get the custom of those collaborators who had clearance to get past the security things, half dog, half bear, knitted together with cybernetic enhancements and armour, that now guarded the diplomatic quarter. However, I seemed to be their only customer, and I suspected that they were relatives of my assiduous guide; for that reason I never left a tip. That day, two days after the party, I was sitting as usual in a wire frame chair, sipping from a bulb of dark strong coffee and nibbling a meltingly sweet *pain au chocolat*, looking out

17
••

across the vista of Paris's main dome while I waited for my guide.

Before the Quiet War, Paris, Dione, was one of the loveliest cities in the solar system, and the largest of all the cities on Saturn's moons. Its glassy froth of domes and tunnels and tents straddled a ridge of upthrust brecciated basalt between Romulus and Remus craters. Since the twin craters are close to the equator of the icy moon's sub-Saturnian hemisphere, Saturn stood almost directly overhead, cycling through his phases roughly every three days. The city had been renowned for its microgravity architecture, its wide, tree-lined boulevards and parks – much of its population was involved in the biotech industries – its café culture and opera and theatres, and the interlinked parkland blisters that stepped down the terraces of Remus crater along the waterfall-filled course of what had been renamed the Proudhon River during the revolution and now, after the end of the Quiet War and the fall of the barricades, was the Little Amazon – or would be, once the pumps were fixed and the watercourse had been cleared of debris.

The main dome, like many others, had been blown during the bloody end of the siege. It was two kilometres across, bisected by a dry riverbed from east to west and by the Avenue des Étoiles, so-called because of the thousands of lanterns that had hung from the branches of its trees, from north to south, and further divided into segments by boulevards and tramways. Clusters of white buildings stood amongst the sere ruins of parks, while warehouses and offices were packed around its

circumference. Although the civic buildings at its centre were superficially intact, their windows were shattered and their white walls were pockmarked to the third storey by the bullet-holes of the bitter hand-to-hand fighting of the bloody day in which eighty thousand citizens died defending their city from invading troops of the Three Powers Alliance. Every scrap of vegetation in the parks had been killed by exposure to vacuum after the blowout, of course, and now, with the restoration of atmospheric pressure, it was all rotting down to mulch. The air of the plaza where I sat, high above it all, held a touch of that cabbagey stink.

I was woken from my reverie by a light touch on my shoulder, the musk of roses. Demi Lacombe fell, light as a bird, into the wire chair on the other side of the little café table and favoured me with her devastating smile. She wore loose white coveralls; I could not help but notice that her breasts were unbound. I scarcely saw Dev Veeder scowling a dozen metres away, or his squad of burly armoured troopers.

Demi Lacombe's left wrist was wrapped in a pressure bandage; when I expressed my concern, she explained that she had fractured it in a silly accident. 'I over-estimated my ability to jump in this lovely light gravity, and took a bit of a tumble. The clinic injected smart bacteria that will fix up the bone in a couple of days. I've seen this place so many times,' she added, 'but I didn't know that you were its patron, Professor-Doctor.'

'Please, my name is Fredo. Won't you join me in a coffee? And you too, perhaps, Colonel Veeder?'

'There's no time for that,' Veeder said brusquely. 'You're a fool to patronise these people, Graves.'

Inside the guardhouse's half-collapsed shroud, the old couple who ran the makeshift café shrank from his black glare.

I said boldly, 'The psychologists tell me that enterprises like this are a healthy sign, Colonel. Even though it is, admittedly, on a microeconomic scale.'

'You're being scammed,' Veeder said. 'I think I ought to re-examine the credentials of your so-called guide.'

'History shows us, Colonel, that those defeated benefit from subsequent cultural and economic fertilisation. Besides, my sponsors would be unhappy if you disturbed my work.'

Demi Lacombe said, 'I think it's a nice thing, Dev. A little sign of reconciliation.'

'Whatever. Come on. It's a long way to the tramhead.'

'The trams are working again?'

'One or two,' Dev Veeder said.

'Dev restored the tram lines which pass through some of the parklands,' Demi said. 'It really does help my surveys.' For a moment, she took my hand in both of hers. 'You're a kinder man than you seem, Fredo,' she said, and floated up out of her chair and took Dev Veeder's arm.

I watched them cross the plaza to the escalators. Demi had only been in Paris a couple of weeks, but she had already mastered the long loping stride which worked best in Dione's low gravity. Only when they had descended out of sight did I look at the scrap of paper she had thrust into my palm.

I must talk with you.

My guide arrived hardly a minute later; I suspected that he had been watching the whole thing from a safe vantage. I suppose I should tell you something about Lavet Corso. The most important thing was that I never entirely trusted him, an instinctive reaction to which I should have paid more attention. But who does like collaborationists? They are despised by their own people for being traitors, and for the same reason are distrusted by those they are so eager to please.

Lavet Corso had once been something in the lower echelons in the city's government, and was studiedly neutral about Marisa Bassi. Although he had arranged many interviews, I had never tried to interview him. He had been widowed in the war and had to support a young daughter in difficult circumstances. While interviewing survivors of the siege, I had to endure the squalor of the warrens in which they lived. On my first visit, Corso had had the temerity to complain about the noise, lack of privacy, dirt and foul air, and I had told him sharply, 'You and your daughter are lucky. Fate saved you from a horrible death. If not for a chance which separated you from your wife, you could have been aboard that scow too. You could have fallen inside a tin can into Saturn's poisonous atmosphere, choking and boiling and flattened in the calorific depths. But you, Mr Corso, were spared, as was your daughter. Life goes on.'

I don't think he took my little homily to heart, but he didn't dare complain again.

Corso was a tremendously tall man, with a pock-

21

marked face, dark eyes and black hair slicked back from his pale face with heavy grease. He was efficient and smarter than he mostly allowed himself to appear; perhaps too smart, for his flattery never seemed sincere, and he was too ready to suggest alternatives to my plans. That day, for instance, after I had told him where I wanted to go, he immediately proposed visiting another sector that was both easier to reach and in a far safer condition.

'It is my life if you are hurt, boss.'

'I hardly think so, given the waivers I had to sign in order to do my fieldwork.'

'And you have been there already, boss. Several times. Very badly damaged it is, not safe at all. And there are still many booby traps.'

'I do remember, Mr Corso, and I also remember that on each occasion you tried to dissuade me. But I will go again, because it is important to me. If we do get into trouble, the machines of the security force claim to be only five minutes away from any spot in the city.'

'It's certainly what we're told,' Corso said. 'Perhaps it's even true.'

'Then lead on, Mr Corso. I want to see this place today.'

A few minutes later, the whole of the main dome was spread beneath us. I sat behind Corso as he laboured at the pedals of the airframe, beneath the central joint of its wide, vivid yellow bat wings. I found this mode of travel quite exhilarating, for Corso was an expert pilot, and in Dione's meagre gravity we could fall a hundred metres and escape with only bruises and perhaps a broken bone or two.

We swooped out above the cankerous, rotting tangles of parks, above streets dotted with half-cleared barricades, above white buildings and the blackened shells of buildings set afire in the last hours of the siege. One reason for the blowout had been to save Paris from its crazed citizens (riding behind Corso, with cold cabbagey air blowing around me, I could imagine the dome's blister filling with swirling fumes, a smoky pearl that suddenly cleared when its integrity was breached; its huge diamond panes were still smudged with the residue of the suddenly snuffed fires). And then the little flying machine stooped and we bounced once, twice, and were down, taxiing across a wide flat roof above an avenue lined with dead chestnut trees.

I had come here on my second day in Paris. I had insisted, and Dev Veeder had, with ill-grace, provided an escort. I had returned several times since, for here were the ruins of the office building, like a broken tooth in the terraced arcades of this commercial sector, from which Marisa Bassi had run his revolutionary committee. Since I had first visited the place, I had learned much more about those desperate, last days. From one of these terraces, bareheaded and in shirt-sleeves, Bassi had made his crucial speech to the crowds who had packed the stilled pedways and empty tram tracks. It was at an intersection nearby that he had organised the first of the barricades, and inaugurated the block captain system by which the building and defence of each barricade was assigned to platoons of a dozen or so citizens. How proud the survivors still were of their token efforts, singing out

the names of the barricades on which they had served
like captains recalling the names of their ships.

Place de la Concorde.

The Killing Field.

The Liberty Line.

For a long time, I stood at the remains of that first
barricade and tried to imagine how it had been, that day
when Bassi had made his speech. To insert myself, by
imaginative reconstruction built on plain fact, into the
life of another, is the most delicate part of my work. As I
stood there, I imagined the chestnut trees in leaf, the heat
and brilliant light of hundreds of suspensor lamps beneath the roof of the dome, like floating stars against the
blackness of Dione's night, the restless crowd in the wide
avenue, faces turned like flowers towards Marisa Bassi.

An immigrant, he was half the height of most of the
population of Paris, but was broad-shouldered and muscular, with a mane of grey hair and a bushy beard woven
through with luminescent beads. What had he felt? He
was tired, for he had certainly not slept that night. I was
certain that he had had a direct hand in the deaths of his
former government colleagues, and perhaps he was
haunted by the bloody scenes. Murder is a primal event.
Did the screams of his murdered colleagues fill him with
foreboding, did his hands tremble as he grasped the rail
and squared his shoulders and prepared to address the
restless crowd? He had showered, and his hair was still
wet as he let go of the rail and raised his hands (I had a
photograph of his hands which I looked at often: they
were square-palmed, the fingers short and stout, with

broken nails – a labourer's rather than a murderer's hands) to still the crowd's noise, and began to speak. And in that moment changed history, and condemned most of his audience to a vainglorious death. Had he planned his speech, or did it come unprompted? Several of those I had interviewed said that he had seemed nervous; several others that he had spoken with flawless confidence; all said that he had spoken without notes, and that he had been cheered to the echo.

I walked about for an hour, every now and then dictating a few words to my notebook, impressions, half-realised ideas. Bassi did not yet stand before me fully-fleshed, but I felt that he was growing closer.

One of the killing machines that patrolled the repressurised parts of the city stalked swiftly across a distant intersection, glittering and angular, like a praying mantis made of steel, there one moment, gone the next. I wondered if it or one of its fellows had caught the man who had painted the silly slogan, *He Lives!*, across the sooty stone of the building's first setback; I would have to ask Dev Veeder.

I told Corso, 'I'm pleased to see that our angels of mercy are afoot.'

'They might reassure you, boss, but they scare the shit out me. I've seen what those things can do to a man.'

'But not to you, my dear Corso. Not while you are under my protection.'

'Not while I have the stink of occupation upon me.'

'That's putting it crudely,' I said.

All of the occupation force and certain of its favoured collaborators had been tweaked so that their sweat emitted specific long-chain lipids that placated the primitive brains of the security things and killing machines.

'I'm sorry, boss. This place weirds me out.'

'Bad memories, perhaps?'

I was wondering if Corso had been there, that day, but as usual, he did not rise to the bait. He said, 'I was on corpse detail, right after they repressurised this part of the city. The bodies had lain in vacuum at minus two hundred degrees centigrade for more than two months. They were shrivelled and very dry. Skin and flesh crisp, like pie crust. It was hard to pick them up without a finger or a hand or a foot breaking off. We all wore masks and gloves, but flakes of dead people got in your skin, and pretty soon all you could smell was death.'

'Don't be so gloomy, Corso. When the reconstruction is finished, your city will have regained its former glory.'

'Yeah, but it won't be my city any more. So, where do you want to go next?'

'To the sector where he lived, of course.'

'Revisiting all your old favourites today, boss?'

'I feel that I'm getting closer to him, Mr Corso.'

We climbed back up to the roof, took off with a sudden stoop, and then, with Corso pedalling furiously, rose high above roofs and avenues and dead parkland.

'I don't understand why you aren't grateful for the reconstruction, Mr Corso. We could quite easily have demolished your city and started over. Or pulled out entirely, and brought you all back to Earth.'

'I was born here. This is where I was designed to live. Earth would kill me.'

'And you *will* live here, thanks to the generosity of the Three Powers Occupation Force, but you will live here as part of the human mainstream. The high flown nonsense about colonising the outer limits of the solar system, the comets and the Kuiper Belt, all of that was sheer madness. I have a colleague who has demonstrated that it is economically impossible. There will be a few scientific outposts, perhaps, but the outer system is too cold and dark and energy poor. It's no place to live. Here though, will be the jewel of Earth's reconciliation with her children, Mr Corso. I believe that the Quiet War will mark the beginning of the first mature epoch of human history, a war to end wars, and an end to childish expansionism. In its place will be as fine a flowering in the sciences and the arts as humanity has ever known. We are lucky to be alive at this time.'

'The Chinese might disagree. About an end to war.'

'Such disagreements as there are between the Democratic Union of China and the Three Powers Alliance will be settled by diplomacy and the intermingling of trade and culture. Men live for so long now that their lives are too valuable to be wasted in war.'

Pedalling hard, Corso said over his shoulder, 'Old men have always used that as an excuse to send young men to war.'

'You are a cynic, Mr Corso.'

'Maybe. Still, it's funny how the war started because

we wouldn't repay our debts, and now you're pouring money into reconstruction.'

How do wars start? I suppose you could graph the rise in government debt against public resentment at the colonies funded by Earth's taxes until a trigger point was reached, a crisis which had finally forced the governments of the Three Powers Alliance to act. That crisis was generally agreed to be the refusal by certain colonies to pay increased rates of interest on the corporate and government loans that had funded their expansion, an act of defiance which coincided with the death of the president of Greater Brazil close to an election, and the need by his inexperienced and unpopular vice president to be seen to act decisively. By that view, the Quiet War was no more than an act of debt recovery. Or perhaps one might suggest that the Quiet War was an historical inevitability, the usual reaction of colonies that had chafed under the yoke of an over-stretched and under-funded empire until they could not help but demand independence: there were dozens of precedents for this in Earth's history.

And yet the colonists had lost. The Three Powers Alliance had the technological and economic advantage, and superior access to information; the colonies, fragile bubbles of air and light and heat scattered in the vastness of the outer solar system, were horribly vulnerable. Apart from a few assassinations and acts of sabotage, almost no one had died on Earth during the Quiet War, but hundreds of thousands had died in the colonies on the moons of Jupiter and Saturn, in orbital habitats and in spacecraft.

Sartre wrote that because of technology we can no longer make history; instead, history is something that happens to us. It is an irony, I suppose, that Marisa Bassi's spark of defiance was extinguished because the very technology which sustained his city made it so very vulnerable.

And yet certain important corporados were sufficiently worried about the futile resistance led by that one man, in one city on one of Saturn's small icy moons, to have sent me to profile him, as a police psychologist might profile a mass murderer.

Was Marisa Bassi a great man who had risen from obscurity to fame but had failed? Or was he a fool, or worse than a fool – a psychopath who had hypnotised an emotionally vulnerable population and made them martyrs not for the cause of liberty, but for gratification of his inadequate ego?

I still had too little material to make that judgment, and I confess that on that day, as I returned to places I had already trawled over, my mind was as much on the implications of Demi Lacombe's note as my work, and to Lavet Corso's undisguised relief I brought an early end to my labours.

Four

It was not easy to arrange a private meeting with Demi Lacombe, for the diplomatic quarter was small, and Dev Veeder's already keen eye was sharpened further by jealousy. I took to walking in the parkland after dark, even though I gave little credence to Cris DeHon's gossip, but I met only tame animals and, once, one of the gardeners, who for a moment gazed at me with gentle, mild curiosity before shambling away into the shadows beneath the huge, shaggy puffballs of a stand of cypress trees.

I spent the next few days within the diplomatic quarter, interviewing wretches caught up in Dev Veeder's latest security sweep. They were either sullen and mostly silent, or effusively defiant, and in the latter case their answers to my questions were so full of lies or boasts or blusters that it was almost impossible to find any grain of truth. One wild-eyed man, his face badly bruised, claimed to have seen Bassi shot in the head in the last moments of the resistance, after the invading troops had blown the main dome and stormed the barricades. Several said that he was sleeping deep beneath one of the moon's icefields, and

would waken again in Paris's hour of need – something I had heard many times already, unconsciously echoing the Arthurian legend just as the Bassi's revolution had so very consciously echoed the Parisian communes of the 19th Century (in our age, all revolutionaries worth their salt must pay fastidious attention to precedent).

All worthless, yet I felt that I was growing near to understanding him. Sometimes he was in my dreams. But suddenly my work no longer mattered, for I contrived my rendezvous with Demi Lacombe.

It was at another of the receptions with which the small community within the diplomatic quarter bolstered its sense of its own worth. It was easily done. By an arrangement I was later to regret, Cris DeHon diverted Dev Veeder into a long and earnest conversation with a visiting journalist about the anti-reconstruction propaganda that was circulating in the general population (in truth no more than a few scruffy leaflets and some motile slogans planted more to irritate the occupying troops than rally the vestigial resistance, but how Dev preened before the journalist's floating camera). I exchanged a glance with Demi Lacombe, and she set her bulb of wheat frappé on a floating tray and set off past the striped tents erected in the airy glade into the woods beyond. I followed a minute later, my heart beating as quickly and lightly as it had when I had set off on romantic assignations half a century ago.

Ferns grew head-high beneath the frothy confections of the trees, but I glimpsed Demi's pale figure flitting through the green shadows and hurried on into the

depths of the ravine which split the quarter's parkland. We soon left the safety of the trees behind but still she went on and I had to follow, although my eagerness was becoming tempered with a concern that we would be spotted by one of the security things.

Yet how wonderful it was, to be chasing that gorgeous creature! We flew down a craggy rock face like creatures in a dream, over vertical fields of brilliantly coloured tweaked orchids, along great falls of ferns and vines and air-kelp. Birds lazily swam in the air; beyond the brilliant stars of suspensor lamps, beyond the diamond panes of the quarter's tent, Saturn blessed us with his pale, benign gaze.

The chase ended in a triangular meadow of emerald-green moss, starred with the spikes of tiny red flowers and backed by the tall, ferny cliff of black, heat-shocked basalt down which we had swum. There was a steep drop to the dark lake at the bottom of the ravine at one edge, and a dense little wood of roses grown as tall as trees at the other. The wild heady scent of the roses did nothing to quieten my heart; nor did the way Demi pressed her hands over mine. The bandage on her left wrist was gone; those smart bacteria had worked their magic.

'Thank you, Fredo,' she said. 'Thank you for this. If I couldn't get away from him now and then I swear I would go crazy.'

How can I describe what she looked like in that moment? Her silvery hair unbound about her heart-shaped face, which was mere centimetres from my own. Her pale, gauzy trousers and blouson floating about her

body. Her scent so much like the scent of the wild roses. The viridescent light of that little meadow, filtered through ferns and roses, gave her pale skin an underwater cast; she might have been a nereid indeed, clasping a swooning sailor to her bosom.

'Dev Veeder,' I said stupidly.

'He's declared his love for me.'

'You must be careful how you respond. You may think him foolish, but it will be dangerous to insult his honour.'

'It's so fucked up,' the gorgeous creature declared. She let go of my hands and strode the width of the meadow in four graceful strides, came back to me in four more. 'I can't *work*, the way he follows me around everywhere.'

'His devotion is exceptional. I take it that you do not reciprocate his infatuation.'

'If you mean do I love him, do I want to marry him, no. No. I thought I liked him, but I knew better than to sleep with him because I know what a big thing it is with you Greater Brazilians.'

I thought then that it might have been better if she had slept with him as soon as possible, since it would have instantly devalued her in Dev Veeder's eyes. She would have become his mistress, but never his wife.

Demi said, 'I think he's been out here too long. I've heard dreadful stories about him.'

'Well, we have been at war.'

'That he tortures his prisoners,' she said. 'That he enjoys it.'

'He is a soldier. Sometimes it is necessary to do things in war that would be unforgivable in peacetime.'

I did not particularly want to defend Dev Veeder, but I did not yet know what she wanted of me, and I was feeling an old man's caution.

'He enjoys it,' she said again.

'Perhaps he enjoys carrying out his duty.'

'A Jesuitical distinction if ever I heard one.'

'I was educated by them, as a matter of fact.'

'So was I! Just outside Dublin. A horrible grey pile of a place that smelled of damp and floor polish and cheap disinfectant. Brr,' she said, and shuddered and smiled. 'I bet you had to endure that lecture on damnation and eternity. The sparrow flying from one end of the Universe to the other . . .'

'On each circuit carrying away in its beak a grain of rice from a mountain as tall as the Moon's orbit.'

'In our lecture the mountain was made of sand. And I guess your priests were men, not women. I still remember the punchline. Even when the sparrow had finished its task not one moment of eternity had passed. They knew how to leave a mark on your soul, the Jesuits. I learned to hate them because they scared me into being good.'

'I am sure that you needed little tuition in that direction, Dr Lacombe.'

'Demi, Fredo. Call me Demi. Quit being so formal.'

'Demi, then.'

'They gave me a strong sense of duty too, the Jesuits. I came here to do a job. An important job.'

I began to understand what she wanted. I said, 'Dev Veeder's attentions are interfering with your work.'

'He's an impossible man. He says that he wants to help me, but he won't listen when I try to tell him that he could best help by letting me get on with my work on my own.'

'He is from a good family. Very old-fashioned.'

'Right. He insists on going everywhere with me, and insists that I stay locked up in the quarter when he can't spare the time to escort me. So I'm way behind in my survey. I mean, I knew it would be a big job, but Dev is making it impossible. And it's so important that it gets done. This was such a wonderful place, before the war.' She made a sweeping gesture that took in the roses, the falls of ferns, the viridescent moss. 'It was all like this, then.'

'The restoration is an important symbol of political faith.'

'Well, there's that. But this city was a biotech showpiece before the war. It had more gene wizards than any other colony, and they exported their expertise to almost everywhere else in the outer system. There's so much we can learn from what's left, and so much more we can learn during the reconstruction.'

'And of course you want to play a part in that. It would set the cap on your career.'

'It was like a work of art,' Demi Lacombe said. 'It would be a terrible sin not to try and restore it. There's a man I need to see. Away from Dev.'

'One of the survivors.'

'Yani Hakaiopulos. He was a gene wizard, once upon a time. As great a talent as Sri Hong-Owen or Avernus. He retired a long time ago, but he helped entrain the basic ecological cycles that underpinned everything else. I can learn so much from him, if I'm given the chance.'

'But he won't talk if Dev Veeder is with you.'

'The Parisians think that Dev is a war criminal.'

'If they had won the war, perhaps that's what he would have become. But they did not.'

'Will you help me, Fredo? You go out into the city alone. You interview the people there.'

'And you want me to interview this man about the city's ecosystems? I would not know where to begin.'

'No,' Demi Lacombe said, her gaze bright and bold. 'I want you to take me with you.'

'Without Dev Veeder's knowledge.'

'Under his nose.'

'He is the chief of police, Demi. No one can come and go without his knowledge.'

'I think I've found a way,' Demi Lacombe said. She stepped back and put two fingers between her blood-red lips and whistled, a single shrill note so loud it startled me, and disturbed a flock of small brown birds which had been perching in the ferns overhead. As they tumbled through the air, a man stepped out of the roses on the other side of the small meadow.

My heart gave a little leap, tugged by guilt, and I was suddenly aware of how much like illicit lovers Demi Lacombe and I must have looked. But the man was no

man at all, merely one of the gardeners, the tutelary spirits of the parkland.

Before the revolution, before the Quiet War, the government of Paris, Dione was an attempt to revive the quaint notion of technodemocracy, an experiment in citizen participation that on Earth had been dismissed long ago as just another utopian idea that was simply too unwieldy in practice. But it had briefly flourished in the little goldfish bowl of the colony city; every citizen could put a motion to change any aspect of governance providing he could enlist a quorum of supporters, and the motion would be enforced by the appropriate moderating committee if a sufficient majority voted it through.

It was a horrible example of how lazy and misguided rulers, who should have been elevated above the mob by virtue of breeding or ability, devolve their natural obligations to ignorance, prejudice and the levelling force of popular taste. Imagine the time wasted in uninformed debate over trivial issues, the constant babble of prejudices masquerading as opinion or even fact! It had been a society shaped not by taste or intelligence but by a kind of directionless, mindless flailing reminiscent of Darwinian evolution. We have mastered evolution, and we must be masters of the evolution of our civilisation, too. Yet Paris's nascent technodemocracy had thrown up one or two interesting ideas, and one of these was its method of capital punishment.

Like all democracies, it mistakenly believed in the essential perfectibility of all men, and so practised rehabilitation of its criminals rather than punishment. But

even it had to admit that there were some criminals who, by genetic inheritance, parental conditioning or choice, were irredeemable. As thrifty as the rest of the energy- and resource-poor colonies of the outer solar system, Paris did not waste material and labour in constructing prisons for these wretches; nor did it waste their potential for labour by executing them. Instead, they were loboto- mised and fitted with transducer and control chips, transforming psychopaths into useful servants, meat ex- tensions of the control system that maintained the park- lands and wilderness and farms of the city.

The gardener Demi had summoned from his hiding place had obviously been an untweaked immigrant, for he was no taller than me. Like the gardener I had en- countered when wandering the parkland like a lorn, lovesick fool, hoping to encounter Demi Lacombe, he was sturdy, barechested and barefoot, his white trousers ragged, his shaven head scarred by the operation which had transformed him, encircled by a coppery headband into which was woven a high-gain broad band antenna. Through this he was linked to both his fellows and the computers which controlled the climate of the parkland, its streams, its hidden machines, and even its animals, which all were fitted with control chips too. Several of the small brown birds that had fallen from the ferns fluttered about his head, calling in high excited voices, unnerv- ingly like those of small children, before flying away over the edge of the meadow. With a rustling and snapping of canes, a pygmy mammoth emerged from the roses, its long russet hair combed straight and gleaming with oils,

its trunk flexed at its broad forehead as the sensitive pink tip snuffled the air. Tools and boxes hung on its flanks, attached to a rope harness.

The gardener scarcely glanced at me; his attention was on Demi Lacombe. I thought I saw a look pass between them, crackling with a shared emotion. Desire, I thought, and in that moment unknowingly sealed her fate, for I was suddenly, violently, unreasonably jealous of the poor child of nature she had summoned, believing that Cris DeHon's malicious insinuations may have been right all along.

'He knows me,' Demi Lacombe said softly. 'I can speak with him.'

'Anyone can speak to them,' I said. 'I understand they are programmed to understand a few simple commands. But mostly they keep away from the people they serve. It's better that way.'

Demi Lacombe smiled and touched her left temple with her forefinger. 'I mean that I can truly talk with him. I have an implant similar to his, so that I can access the higher functions of the machines which control the habitat. Through them, I can talk with him. Watch, Fredo! I can send him away as easily as I summoned him.'

She made no signal, but the gardener turned and parted the canes of the roses and vanished into them. The mammoth turned too and trotted after him. It was unnervingly like magic, and I briefly wondered how else she might have commanded the brute, before crushing the vile image as a man might crush a loathsome worm beneath the heel of his boot.

Demi said, 'He showed me a way out of here that Dev and his troopers don't know about.'

I laughed, a trifle excessively I fear. I was not quite myself. Roses in a wild garden, a woman trapped by her own beauty, a compliant monster. I said, 'Really, Demi. A secret passage?'

'A stream was diverted when the layout of the parkland was redesigned twenty years ago. Its sink pipe wasn't sealed up because it lies at the bottom of the lake, down there.' She stepped gracefully to the edge of the meadow. A light wind blew up the face of the cliff, stirring her long, silvery hair as she pointed downwards; she looked like a warrior from some pre-technological myth.

I shuffled carefully to her side, and looked down at the long, narrow sleeve of black water that was wedged at the bottom of the ravine, between the base of the cliff on which we stood and the wall of bare sheetrock that rose in huge bolted slabs towards the foot of one of the tent's diamond panes, high above us.

Demi said, 'The pipe is flooded, but the gardeners can give me one of the air masks they wear when they clean out the bulk storage tanks. There's a pressure gate that must be opened – it fell closed when the main dome was blown. Then I'll be outside.'

'It sounds dangerous. More dangerous than Dev Veeder.'

'I've tested the pressure gate. I know it works. But I need help getting across the main part of the city.' She had turned to me, her face shining with excitement. How

young she was, how lovely! Her scent was very strong at that moment; I could have drowned in it quite happily. She said, 'I need your help, Fredo. Will you help me?'

For a moment, I quite forgot my loathsome spasm of jealousy. 'Of course,' I said. 'Of course I will, my dear Demi. How could I refuse the plea of a maiden in distress?'

We made our plans as we walked back through the shaggy exuberances of the cypresses towards the lights and noise of the party. We took care to return to it separately, from different directions, but still my heart gave a little leap when I saw Dev Veeder moving purposefully through knots of chattering people, hauling himself hand over hand along one of the waist-high tethers that webbed the lawn. He was making straight for Demi, and when he reached her she put her hand on his shoulder and her lovely, delicate face close to his and talked quietly into his ear. He nodded and smiled, and she smiled too, my cunning minx.

'Now you can tell me all about it.'

I swung around so quickly that I would have floated above the heads of the chattering party-goers if Cris DeHon had not caught my wrist. The neuter's fingers were long and delicate, and fever-hot. It wore a white blouson slashed here and there to show flashes of scarlet lining, as if it were imitating the victim of some primitive and bloody rite. Its hair was dyed a crisp white, and stiffened in little spikes.

'Tell me all about it,' DeHon said. 'What plot's afoot? Is it love?'

I smiled into the neuter's sharp pale face. 'Don't be ridiculous.'

'A marriage of summer and winter is not unknown. And if you're half the distinguished scholar you claim to be, you'd be quite a catch for a struggling academic from the most backward and impoverished country of the Alliance.'

'She was showing me some of the wonders of our gardens,' I said, shaking free of DeHon's hot grasp. 'This city is famous for its gene wizards.'

DeHon smiled craftily, looking sidelong through the crowd at Demi Lacombe and Dev Veeder. 'I don't believe it for a minute, but I won't spoil the fun. The curtain has risen; the play has commenced. For your sake, I hope Dev Veeder will be in a good temper when he discovers your little plot.'

The night passed in a daze of half-sleeping, half-waking. I had never slept well in Dione's light gravity, and what sleep I had that night was full of murky dreams coloured by fear and desire.

The next morning, I drank an unaccustomed second cup of coffee at the makeshift café, and when Lavet Corso finally arrived, I instructed him to fly us to the coordinates that Demi Lacombe had given me.

He stared at me insolently, the seams in his face tightening around his mouth. 'That's nothing but a park, boss.'

'Nevertheless, that is where we will go.'

And so we did, after a brief argument which I quite enjoyed, and which did more to wake me than the coffee did. I was beginning to suspect that Corso's protests were ritual, like the bargaining one must do in a souk when making a purchase. Now that the game was afoot, I was in a careless mood of anticipation, and did not complain at the pitch and yaw of the airframe as Corso slipped it through updraughts, spiralling down to the brown and black wreckage of the park.

We swooped in low over the tops of skeletal trees which raised their white arms high above a wasteland of deliquescing vegetation. The stink was horrible. An eye of water gleamed in the shadow of a low cliff of raw basalt, and a small figure stepped from a cleft at the foot of the cliff and semaphored its arms. A flood of relief and renewed desire turned my poor foolish heart quite over. I tapped Corso's shoulder, but he had already seen her. The wings of the airframe boomed as they shed air, and we skidded across a black carpet of mulch.

Demi Lacombe floated down from the cleft, from which a little water still trickled into what had once been a lake, and ran to us with huge loping strides, sleek in silvery skinthins that hugged every contour of her slim body. An airmask and a small tank dangled from one hand. Her wet hair was snarled around her beautiful face, made yet more beautiful by the brilliant smile she turned on me.

Corso gave a low whistle, and I said sharply, 'Enough of that. Remember your poor dead wife.'

'You're late,' Demi said breathlessly.

'My guide has a bad sense of time.'

'It doesn't matter. Well, I'm ready. Let's go!'

'You have not brought . . . more suitable attire?'

Demi laughed, and cocked her hip. The silvery material was moulded tightly to every centimetre of her body. 'What's wrong? You don't like this?'

I liked it very much indeed, of course, and it was obvious that Corso did too. He was cranking up the prop, to give enough kinetic energy to assist takeoff. When I told him sharply to hurry up, he mumbled something about overloading.

'Nonsense. You hardly expect my passenger to walk. Look lively! Every moment we stay here risks discovery.'

'I didn't sign up for adventure,' Corso said. He straightened, with one hand to the small of his back. 'Maybe you better tell me what this is all about, boss.'

'You just get us to the warrens,' I said.

'No,' Demi said, 'he's right.' She stepped up to Corso and touched his arm and said, 'You're Lavet Corso, aren't you? Professor-Doctor Graves has told me so much about the help you've given him.'

'And who are you?'

'Dr Demi Lacombe. I'm here to help reconstruct your wonderful ecosystem, and I want to talk to Yani Hakaiopulos.'

'Really,' Corso said, but I could see that he was weakening. 'Why not have your boyfriend haul him in?'

'My boyfriend?'

'Colonel Veeder. You are the woman he's been escorting everywhere.'

'Well, that's true, but he isn't my boyfriend, and that's why I need your help.'

Corso locked the prop's winding mechanism and said, 'You can try and talk to Yani if you like, but you'll find he's immune to your charms. Climb on board now, both of you. Let's see if I can get this higher than the trees.'

Demi looked at the flimsy airframe and said, 'I thought it would be safer to walk.'

'Not at all,' I said. 'It would take several hours, and we would be bound to encounter more than one of the killing machines, and they would report straight back to the security forces. But no one bothers to watch where we go.'

'You had better be right, boss.'

The airframe jinked across the rotten black carpet and bounded into the air. Demi, seated behind me, screamed loudly and happily. She had put her arms around my waist; the pressure of her body against my back, and her musky scent, almost as strong as the cabbage-stink of the rotten vegetation, awakened a part of me that had been sleeping for quite some time.

Although Corso was pedalling hard, the airframe clambered through the middle air of the dome with the grace of a pregnant dragonfly. I leaned back and pointed out to Demi the remains of barricades across the avenues, the ruined hulk of the Bourse, like a shattered wedding cake, where the last of those citizens who had been in or near to pressure suits when the dome had been blown open had made their final stand. Once, I saw the silver twinkle of a killing machine stalking down the middle of the

Avenue des Étoiles; Corso must have seen it too, for he veered the airframe away, scudding in towards one of the flat rooftops clustered around the edge of the dome.

The place was an automated distribution warehouse of some kind, and although it would have been cleared of any bodies, the red-lit echoing emptiness of its storage areas and ramps was eerie. Demi kept close to me as Corso led us down a narrow street. I told her about Marisa Bassi's early days in Paris, Dione, when as an immigrant he had worked in one of these warehouses, rising quickly to become its supervisor, then moving on to become a partner in an import-export business of dubious legality, where he had made enough money to buy his citizenship.

'And two years after that he became a councillor, and then the war came. The rest will be history, once I have written it.'

'Your history, maybe,' Corso said.

'All history belongs to the winners,' I said, 'so it will be your history too. If you know anything about Bassi, now's the time to tell me.'

'Nothing you need to know, boss,' Corso said, with his maddening disingenuousness.

Marisa Bassi had been living in this semi-industrial sector when the war began. Imagine his small, sparsely furnished room that evening, the sounds of the street drifting up through a window open to catch any stray breeze: a tram rattling through a nearby intersection; the conversation of people strolling about as the suspensor lights dimmed overhead; the smell of food from the cafés

and restaurants. Bassi was sitting in a chair, flicking through page after page on his slate – he hated the paperwork that went with his job, and was especially impatient with it now that the first move towards independence had been made – when he heard a distant thump, like a huge door closing. At the same moment the suspensor lights flickered, came back on. Bassi looked out of the window and saw people running, all in one direction, running with huge loping strides like gazelles fleeing a lion's rush. His heart felt hollow for a moment, then filled with a burst of adrenalin. He called out to someone he recognised, and the man stopped and shouted up that it was the parliament building, someone had blown it up.

'It's war!' the man added, holding up a little scrap of TV film. Let's say that he was a Sicilian too, Bep Martino or some such rough hewn name, a construction worker. He and Bassi played chess and drank rough red wine under the chestnut trees in the little park at the end of the street.

'Wait there!' Bassi said. 'I'm coming with you!'

It seemed that most of the population of Paris had converged on the ruins of the parliament building. It had neatly collapsed on itself, its flat roof draped broken-backed across the pancaked remains of its three storeys. People had organised themselves into teams and were carefully picking through the wreckage, chains of men and women passing chunks of fractured concrete from top to bottom, stopping every now and again while someone listened for the calls of those who had been

buried. Living casualties were carried off to hospital; the dead lay in a neat row under orange blankets on the trampled lawns.

Followed by his friend, Marisa Bassi restlessly stalked all the way around the perimeter of the building. Five killed, eighteen injured, a doctor told him, and probably more still to be found in the rubble.

Bep Martino appraised the ruins with a critical eye and said that it was a professional job. 'Charges placed just so, the walls went out and the floors fell straight down. Boom!' Every so often, he flattened out the TV on his palm and gave a report on what it was saying. Earth's three major powers had made good their threat, and were sending out what they called an expeditionary force to quell revolutionary elements in their outer colonies.

'Note the possessive,' Bassi said.

'Well, we voted to suspend payments,' Martino said, 'so I guess we're all revolutionaries now.'

'This is our moment,' Bassi said.

He stopped to talk with another councillor, a third generation tweak, very tall, and thin as a rail. Stooping, he told Bassi that the air conditioning had failed because of a virus, and software faults had shut down the fusion reactors; the city was running on battery power.

'We expected all this,' Bassi said impatiently. 'It is only a warning. We will get the systems back on line, we will clear this up. We will bury our dead and swear on their graves that they will not have died in vain.'

He said this last loudly, for the benefit of the people who were gathering around the two councillors, felt a

gleeful kick of adrenalin, and added, because he liked the phrase, 'This is our moment.'

'We did not expect them to send soldiers,' the tall councillor said gloomily.

'We'll fight if we have to,' Bassi said, his face burning with a sudden self-righteous anger. 'We built this city; no soldiers can take it from us.'

People were clapping and shouting all around him now. The councillor took his elbow and said quietly, 'Be careful of the mob, Bassi. It'll eat you up, if you let it.'

Surely someone would have told him something like that, but with the taste of concrete dust in his throat and his blood up, Marisa Bassi would have shrugged off any advice. It was not a time for moderation or conciliation. That was what he told the city's prime committee a day later, as they debated their response to the threats made by the Three Powers Alliance, and on that day at least, the council was with him, for it agreed to declare a state of war.

The stage was set. Soon, Marisa Bassi would dominate it.

The sector where he had lived was dead now; his entire city was dead. Corso, Demi Lacombe and I crept like mice in a deserted house along a walkway that plunged through the dome's rocky skirt (its diamond panes arching high above us as if we were microbes trapped in a fly's eye). It was one of the many ways into the warrens where the survivors of the city's siege had hidden, walkways and passages and shafts linking insulated dormitories or hydroponic tunnels. One of the walkways

actually ran a little way across the naked face of the ridge, and gave views to the northwest of the dark, rumpled floor of Romulus crater. The moon was so small that the far side of the crater was well below the horizon, and we seemed to be standing on a high, curved cliff looking out across a sea frozen in the midst of a violent tempest. Saturn's banded disc of salmon and saffron was tipped high in the black sky, the narrow arc of his rings shining like polished steel.

There was the landing platform, two shuttles standing on top of it like toys on a cakestand. There were the orange slashes and dashes and squiggles, like ribbons of cuneiform code, of the vacuum organism fields. As I pointed these out to Demi, a huge trembling and translucent jellyfish rose up from the sharply drawn line of the close horizon, its skirts glittering in the harsh sunlight even as it began to lose shape and fall back towards the plain. It was where many of the surviving population of Paris had been put to work, excavating fragments of the iron-rich bolide whose impact had formed the twin craters. I had not finished explaining this when another jellyfish rose, writhing, into the sunlight, and a moment later the tremor of the first explosion passed through the walkway.

I told Demi, 'It is an open-cast mine. They must be making it wider or deeper. The ice is so cold it is hard as rock, and that's why they must use explosives.'

'Means two or three more people will die out there today,' Corso said. 'Or get badly hurt.'

'Don't be impertinent,' I told him. 'It's important work,

necessary work. The metals will aid in the reconstruction of your city.'

'I only mean that Yani might suddenly be too busy to have time to talk to the young lady, boss,' Corso said.

'Keep a civil tongue in your head, Mr Corso, or you might find yourself working in the mines. Or back on corpse detail.'

'It would most likely be the mines,' Corso said, 'seeing as they've mostly cleared away the dead.'

We passed through an antiquated airlock, a sequence of diamond slabs which had to be cranked open and shut by hand, into the noise and squalor and stink of refugee town. It had once been part of the city's farm system, first growing raw organics in the form of unicellular algae, and then, after vacuum organisms had been developed, cultivating fruits and vegetables for the luxury market.

Now, the wide, low-roofed tunnels, mercilessly lit by piped sunlight, divided by panels of extruded plant waste or pressed rock-dust, by blankets or sheets hung from wires and plastic string, were the crude dormitory quarters of the thousand or so surviving Parisians. Although many were off working two- or three-day shifts at the mines or helping to restore the vacuum farms (the city's vacuum organisms had been killed by prions that had catalysed a debilitating change in their photosynthetic pigments, and were slowly being stripped out and replaced), the wretched place seemed noisy and crowded. Everything was damp, and the hot, heavy air was ripe with the smell of sewage and body odour. A dubious brown liquid trickled under the raised slats of the walk-

way down which Corso led Demi and me. He walked several paces ahead of us, with a self-consciousness I'd not seen before, as he led us to the hospital where Yani Hakaiopulos worked.

People were sitting at the openings of their crudely partitioned spaces. A few looked up and, with dull eyes, watched us go by. Old men and women mostly; one crone dandled a fretting baby whose face was encrusted with bloody mucus.

'Poor thing,' Demi whispered to me.

War is cruel, I almost said, but her look of compassion was genuine and my sentiment was not. I had been here many times before to interview the unfortunate survivors about Marisa Bassi, and I confess that my heart had been hardened to the squalor to which their reckless actions had consigned them.

The hospital was another converted agricultural tunnel, beyond yet another set of tiresome mechanically operated doors. The reception area, where a dozen patients waited on stretchers or a medley of plastic chairs, was walled off by scratched and battered transparent plastic scarred with the lumpy seams of hasty welds. Corso talked with a weary woman in a traditional white smock, and was allowed through into the main part of the hospital, where beds stood in neat rows in merciful dimness – in there, the piped sunlight was filtered through beta cloth tacked over the openings in the low ceiling.

Most of the medical orderlies were missionary Redeemers, grey-skinned, tall and skinny, wrapped in bandages

like so many of their patients, or Egyptian mummies come to life. They all had the same face. There were many badly burned patients, immobilised inside moulded plastic casings while damaged skin and muscles were reconstructed. A few people shuffled about, often on crutches; many were missing limbs. Corso passed between the beds into the obscure dimness at the far end of the hospital, and within a minute returned, leading a stooped old man in a white smock spattered with bloodstains. As they came into the reception area, I understood what Corso had meant when he had said that Demi's charms might not work, for Yani Hakaiopulos was blind.

The old gene wizard was congenitally sightless, in fact, having been born with an undeveloped optic chiasma, but he could see, after a fashion. Corso commandeered the hospital's single office, and stuck three tiny cameras to its walls; Yani Hakaiopulos had an implant which transmitted the camera pictures as the sensation of needles on his skin, and so gave him a crude analog of vision. All this Yani Hakaiopulos explained while Corso set up the cameras.

'It hurts to see,' he said, smiling at us one by one when the system had been switched on, 'which is why I do not use it most of the time. Also, I see little more than shapes and movement, and so for my work it is more convenient to use my other senses.'

'A blind doctor!' I exclaimed. 'Now I have seen everything.'

'I am not a qualified doctor, sir,' Yani Hakaiopulos said, 'but in these terrible times even I may be of some help.'

He turned his face in Demi's direction. 'I understand that you have come to talk with me, my dear. I'm flattered, of course.'

'I'm honoured that you would interrupt your work to talk with me,' Demi said.

'There's not much to be done now, except try and keep those well enough to recover from dying of an opportune infection, and to nurse those who are too ill to recover through their last days. And the Redeemers are far better at that than I am. You,' he said, turning his face approximately in my direction, 'I believe that you are the historian. The one who goes around asking people about Marisa Bassi.'

'Did you know him?'

'No, not really. I had been long retired and out of the public eye when the war began, and I could hardly help in the defence of the city. I did meet him once, after his escape from the invaders, in the last hours of our poor city. He came to the hospital – not this one, but the one which lies in ruins in the main dome – to be treated for the gunshot wound he had received, but he was only there for a handful of minutes. A good voice he had. Warm and quiet, but it could fill a room if he let it.'

'He was wounded in the side,' I said.

'Yes,' Yani Hakaiopulos said, and touched the left side of his stained white smock, just under his ribs. The dark, mottled skin of his face was tight on the skull beneath, his teeth large and square and yellow, his white hair combed sideways across a bald pate. He had an abstracted yet

serene air, as if he was happy with the world just as he found it.

I said, 'Some claim that he later died of his wound.'

'I would not know, Professor-Doctor Graves, for I did not treat him.' He turned his smile to Demi and added, 'But I believe you have come here to talk of the future, not the past. I am afraid that I do not give much thought to the future – there's very little of it left for me.'

'I am here to learn,' Demi said, and suddenly knelt down in front of him like a supplicant, and took his hands in hers. She said, in a small, quiet voice, 'I do want to learn. That is, if you will allow it.'

The old man allowed her to bring his fingers to her face. He traced her lips, the bridge of her nose, the downy curve of her cheek. He smiled and said, 'I haven't had a pupil for many years, and besides, I am long out of practice. My small contribution to the greening of the city was made long ago.'

'Knowledge of the past can help remake the future,' Demi said, with fierce ardour.

'Many of my people would say that the city should be destroyed,' Yani Hakaiopulos said.

'They certainly did their best,' I said.

'Yes, indeed. At the end, many were possessed by the idea that they should destroy their city rather than let it fall into the hands of their enemies. They knew that the war was lost, and that if the city survived it would no longer be their city.'

'But it will be,' Demi insisted, 'once it has been rebuilt.'

'No, my dear. It will be like a doppelganger of a dear dead friend, living in that dead friend's house, wearing their clothes.'

Demi sat back, and I was aware once more of the way her slim, full-breasted body moved inside the tight fabric of her silvery skinthins. She said, 'Do you believe that?'

'I do not believe that the great, delicate systems we engineered, the animals and plants we made, can be brought back as they once were. Perhaps something equally wonderful might rise in its place, but I wouldn't know. I'm an old man, the last of the gene wizards. All of my colleagues are dead, from old age, from the war . . .'

'I have studied the parkland in the diplomatic quarter,' Demi said. 'I have talked with its gardeners, walked its paths . . . I think I understand a small part of what this city once possessed.'

Yani Hakaiopulos breathed deeply, then reached out and briefly caressed the side of her face. He said, 'You truly want to do this thing?'

'I want to learn,' Demi said.

'Well, if you can endure an old man's ramblings, I will do my best to tell something of how it was done.'

They talked a long time. An hour, two. I sat outside the office while they talked, and drank weak, lukewarm green tea, with Corso fretting beside me. He was worried that Dev Veeder would learn about our little escapade.

'Go and see your daughter,' I suggested at last, tired of his complaints.

'She's in school, and her teacher is this fierce old woman who does not like her classes disturbed. It's okay

for you, boss. Veeder can't touch you. But if he finds that
I brought his girlfriend here –'

'She isn't his girlfriend.'

'*He* thinks she is.'

'Well, that is true. She is cursed by her beauty, I think.'

'She's dangerous. You be careful, boss.'

'What nonsense, Mr Corso. I'm nearly as old as your
friend Yani Hakaiopulos.'

'He's a great man, boss. And she got him telling her his
secrets almost straight away. It's spooky.'

'Unlike most of you, I think he wants the city rebuilt.'

'Spooky,' Corso said again. 'And she said she was
talking with the gardeners.'

'Oh, that. She has had transducers or the like im-
planted in her brain.' I touched my temples. The knife-
blade of a headache had inserted itself in the socket of my
left eye. The air in the warrens was bad, heavy with
carbon dioxide and no doubt laced with a vile mixture of
pollutants, and the brightly lit reception area was very
noisy. I said, 'She told me that she can interface with the
computers that control the climate of the parklands and
so on. And through them, she can, in a fashion, commu-
nicate with the gardeners. There is no magic about it,
nothing sinister.'

'If you say so, boss,' Corso said. He fell into a kind of
sulk, and barely spoke as he led us back through the
warrens to the main part of the city, and the rooftop
where he had left the airframe.

Six

Dev Veeder found me the next morning at the café, where I was waiting for Lavet Corso to make an appearance. The colonel came alone, sat opposite me and waved off the old man who came out of the half-collapsed guardhouse to ask what he wanted. He seemed amiable enough, and asked me several innocuous questions about the progress of my work.

'I find this Bassi intriguing,' he said. 'A shame he's dead.'

'I hope I might bring his memories to life.'

'Hardly the same thing, Professor-Doctor Graves, if you don't mind my saying so.'

'Not at all. I am quite aware of the limitations of my technique, but alas, there is no better way.'

'It's interesting. He was a fool, an amateur soldier who chose to stand and fight in a hopeless situation, yet he was able to rally the entire population of the city to his cause. But perhaps he was not really their leader at all. Perhaps he was merely a figurehead raised up by the mob.'

'He was certainly no figurehead,' I said. 'The assassination of his fellow members of the government showed

that he was capable of swift and ruthless action. He was tireless in rallying the morale of those who manned the barricades – indeed, when the invasion of Paris began, he was captured at an outlying barricade.'

'The sole survivor amongst a rabble of women and old men. They were fighting against fully armoured troopers with hand weapons, industrial lasers and crude bombs.'

'And he escaped, and went back to fight.'

Dev Veeder thought about that, and admitted, 'I suppose I do like him for that.'

'You do?'

Dev Veeder was staring at me thoughtfully. His dark, almost black eyes were hooded and intense. I had the uncomfortable feeling that he was seeing through my skin. He said, 'Marisa Bassi didn't have to escape. He didn't have to fight on.'

'He would have been executed.'

'Not at all, Professor-Doctor. Once captured, he could have sued for peace. If he truly was the leader of the mob, they would have obeyed him. He would have saved many lives; some might have even been grateful. The Three Powers Alliance wouldn't have been able to install him as head of a puppet government, of course, but they could have pensioned him off, returned him to wherever it was on Earth he was born.'

'Sicily.'

'There you are. He could have opened a pizza parlour, become mayor of some small town, made a woman fat and happy with a pack of bambinos.'

'The last is unlikely, Colonel.'

'But he stuck to the cause he had adopted. He went back. He finished the job. He may have been an amateur and a fool, Professor-Doctor Graves, but he had a soldier's backbone.'

'And caused, as you said, many unnecessary deaths, and much unnecessary destruction.'

I gestured at the devastation spread beyond the foot of the plaza's escalators: the rotting parks; the streets still choked with rubble; the shattered buildings. Dev Veeder did not look at it, but continued to stare at me with a dark, unfathomable intensity.

I made a show of peering at the empty air above the rooftops of the city and said, 'My wretched guide is late.'

'He'll come. He has no choice. This talk interests me, Professor-Doctor. We haven't talked like this for a while.'

'Well, you've been busy.'

'I have?'

'With your new prisoners. And of course, escorting Demi.'

'Dr Lacombe?'

I felt heat rise in my face. 'Yes, of course. Dr Lacombe.'

'Tell me, Professor-Doctor Graves, do you think that Marisa Bassi was one of your great men?'

'His people – those who survive – think that he was.'

'His people. Yes. Do you know, many of them cry out his name in the heat of questioning?'

'I don't see –'

'Usually, those subjected to hot questioning scream for their mothers at the end. When they're emptied, when

61

they've given up everything. Huge bloodied babies shitting and pissing themselves, unable to move because we've broken every major bone, bawling for the only unfailing comfort in all the world. But these people, they cry out for Bassi.' Dev Veeder's right hand made a fist and softly struck the cradle of his left. He wore black gloves of fine, soft leather. One rumour was that they were vat-grown human skin. Another that they were not vat-grown. He said, 'Can you imagine it, Professor-Doctor? You've been broken so badly you know you're going to die. You're flayed open. You've given up everything you've ever loved. Except for this one thing. Your love of the man who led you in your finest hour. You don't give him up. No, in your last wretched moment, you call out to him. You think he'll come and *help* you.'

'That's . . . remarkable.'

'Oh yes. Remarkable. Astonishing. Amazing. What do you think you would call out, if you were put to the question, Professor-Doctor Graves?'

'I'm sure I don't –'

'Nobody knows,' Dev Veeder said, 'until the moment. But I'm sure you'd call for your mother, eh?' His smile was a thing of muscles and teeth, with only cold calculation behind it. 'Was Marisa Bassi a great man? His people think so, and perhaps that's enough.'

I said, eager to grasp this thread, 'He lost his war. Great men are usually remembered because they won.'

'It goes deeper than winning or losing,' Dev Veeder said. 'The important thing is that Bassi took responsibility for his actions. He was captured; he escaped and returned

at once to the fight. Technology makes most men remote from the war they create. At the end of the Second World War, which was, as you know, the first truly modern war, neither the crew of the American aircraft *Enola Gay* nor most of the technicians and scientists who built the atomic bomb, nor even the politicians who ordered its use, none of them felt any guilt over what they did. Why not? The answer is simple: the destruction was remote from them. In the Quiet War, most people were killed by technicians millions of kilometres away. Technicians who fought the war in eight hour shifts and then went home to their spouses and children. Remoteness and division of labour induces both a diminished sense of responsibility and moral tunnel vision, so that men see the task of killing only in terms of efficiency and meeting operation parameters. In my line of work it is different, of course. That is why I am despised by so many, but I believe that I am a more moral man than they for at least I know exactly what I do. I see the fear in my victims' eyes; I smell their sweat and their voided bladders and guts; I get blood on my hands. And I am often the last person they see, so I do not stint my sympathy for their plight.'

I said, 'It must make breaking their bones difficult.'

'Not at all. I do it with a clear conscience because they are the enemy, because it is necessary. But at no time do I reduce them to ciphers or quotients or statistics. They are not targets or casualties or collateral damage. They are men and women in the glory of their final agony. People hate me, yes. But while they think they hate me because

of what I do, in fact they hate me because they see in me what they know is lacking in them. Nietzsche had it right: the weak mass always despises the strong individual.'

I was sure that Nietzsche had said no such thing, and told Dev Veeder, 'Nietzsche tried to erase moral responsibility and went mad doing it. On the morning when they finally had to haul him off to the asylum, he rushed out of his lodgings, still wearing his landlord's nightcap, and tearfully embraced a carthorse. The amoral philosophy which the Nazis would adopt as their own in the Second World War, the creed which would shatter Europe, had already shattered his mind.'

'Do you fear me, Professor-Doctor?'

'Fear? What a question!'

'Because, you know, you should. This place, where you play-act the role of conqueror of the world, it will have to go. It endangers security. I will see to it,' Dev Veeder said, and stood up and bowed and loped away.

I knew that Cris DeHon had betrayed me, but when I returned from my research in the ruins of the city and confronted him, the neuter denied it with an uncomfortable laugh.

'Why should I spoil all the fun?'

'Fun?'

'The plot. The play. The unfolding mysteries of the human heart.'

'You have no right to talk of such things, DeHon. You opted out of all that.'

DeHon clutched its breast dramatically. 'A cruel cut, Graves. I may be desexed, but I'm still human, and part of

life's great comedy. If nothing else, I can still watch. And I do like to watch.'

'Nevertheless, you told him.'

'I won't deny that our gallant love-struck colonel asked me if I knew where his sweetheart had been while I was talking with him at that party. You still owe me for that, by the way.'

'Not if you told him.'

'Perhaps I did let a little something slip. Please, don't look at me that way! I didn't mean to, but our colonel is very persistent. It is his job, after all.'

The small, bright-eyed smile with which this admission was delivered let me know that DeHon had deliberately revealed something about the assignation to Dev Veeder. I said, 'It was innocent. Quite innocent.'

'I do not believe,' DeHon said, 'that Demi Lacombe is as innocent as she likes people to think she is.'

This was at a reception held by the Pacific Community's trade association. Several of its companies had just won the contract to rebuild Dione's organic refineries. Most of us were there. Dev Veeder was standing to one side of a group of biochemists who were talking to Demi Lacombe. He saw me looking at him, and raised his bulb of wine in an ironic salute.

When I had returned to the plaza that afternoon, I had found that Dev Veeder had been true to his word. The café was gone, its mismatched chairs and tables and the shell of the half-ruined guardshouse cleared away. Later, I discovered that the old man and woman who had run it had been sent to work in the vacuum organism fields, a

virtual death sentence for people their age, but I did not need to know that to understand that Dev Veeder had made his point, and I managed to have a brief word with Demi at the buffet of sushi, seaweed, and twenty varieties of bananas stewed and fried and stuffed – exotic food shipped from Earth at God knows what expense for our delectation.

As I transferred morsels I would not eat from the prongs of the serving plates to the prongs of my bowl, I told Demi, 'He knows.'

'He doesn't know. If he did, he would have done something.'

'He *has* done something,' I said, and told her about the café. Had I known then about the fate of its proprietors I would not have dared to even speak with her.

She said, 'I'm going again tomorrow. If you are too scared to help me, Professor-Doctor Graves, I will find my own way across the city.'

With a pang of jealousy, I thought of the way that Yani Hakaiopulos's fingers had caressed her face. The two of them sharing secrets while I waited outside like a court eunuch. I said, 'Colonel Veeder will be watching you.'

'He has to make a presentation about security to company representatives, and I've told him that I will be working in the diplomatic quarter's parkland.' She touched her temple. 'If his men do try to follow me in there, and so far they have not, I'll see them long before they see me. And I know you won't tell him, Fredo. But we shouldn't talk any more, or at least, not here. I think Dev is getting suspicious.'

'He is more than suspicious,' I said. My cheeks were burning like those of a foolish adolescent. 'And that is why, I am afraid, I can no longer help you.'

I did not go into the city the next day, for if I did I knew that I would have to go back to that ruined park and wait for Demi to emerge from the cliff, like Athena stepping new-born from the brow of Zeus. If nothing else, I still had my pride. She will need my help, I thought, and I was wounded when, of course, she did not seek me out.

The day passed, and the next, and still she did not come. I discounted the third day because she was taken out into the city by Dev Veeder; but on the morning of the fourth, hollow, anxious, defeated, I summoned Lavet Corso and ordered him to fly me straight to the ruined park.

He knew what I was about, of course; I made no pretence about it. We landed on the black slime of the lawn, and I saw a rill of water falling from the cleft in the black basalt cliff and felt my heart harden.

'Take me back,' I told Corso.

'Sure, boss, but I'll have to wind the prop first.'

While he worked, I said, 'You knew all along, didn't you?'

'A woman like that coming down to the warrens, well, she's hard to miss, boss.'

'I suppose that she is talking with that gene wizard. With Yani Hakaiopulos.'

'I don't like it either, boss.'

'You were right about her, Mr Corso. She uses men. Even old fools like me and your Mr Hakaiopulos. There

was a school of thought in the late Twentieth Century that men – even great men – were ruled by their genitals. They couldn't help themselves, and as a result they either treated all women like prostitutes, or the women who were involved in their lives had an undue influence on them. It's long been discredited, but I wonder if there isn't some truth to it. We can never really know what is in the hearts of men, for after all, most refuse to admit it to themselves. At least your own great man, Marisa Bassi, was not troubled by women. The sector where he went looking for sex . . .'

'The Battery?'

'Yes, you took me there. One must admire, I suppose, the meticulousness of city planners who would design a neighbourhood where men can go to find other men, free of class, driven only by desire.'

'It wasn't really designed, boss. It sort of grew up. And it wasn't just gay men who went there.'

'Do you think he went there while he was organising the resistance to the siege?'

'I wouldn't know, boss.'

'No, of course not. You did not know him, as you keep reminding me, and you are a family man. But I expect that he did. Leaders of men are almost always highly sexed. We can't condemn such impulses.'

Corso locked the crank of the prop and stood back, dusting his hands. 'You're not just talking about Marisa Bassi now, are you?'

'No. No, I suppose not. It's all part of the human comedy . . . or tragedy.'

'We can go now, boss. It's all wound up and waiting.'

'Of course. Then take me back to the quarter, Mr Corso. I think I must tell Colonel Veeder about this security problem.'

Corso paused, halfway through swinging into the pilot's sling. One hand was raised, grasping a support strut of the airframe's wide canary yellow wings, and half his face was in shadow. He gave me a level, appraising look and said, 'Are you sure you want to do that?'

'The security of the diplomatic quarter is at risk. It's not only Demi Lacombe who could be using that way in and out of the parklands.' When Corso did not reply, I bent and touched the bulge of the blazer, holstered at my calf. 'Get me back, Mr Corso. I insist.'

'You will get more people than her into trouble, boss.'

'I will tell Colonel Veeder that your part in this was blameless. That you were under my orders.'

'I'm not just thinking of myself.'

'Yani Hakaiopulos will have to take his chance. I shudder to think what Demi must have done, to gain his secrets.'

'I think it's more a question of what she did to him,' Corso said.

'I have had enough of your impertinence, Mr Corso. Look sharp, now. I want to get this whole unfortunate business over with.'

'I don't think so, boss.'

'What?'

He let go of the strut and stepped back and said flatly, 'It won't take you long to walk back, even if you have to use

69

the stairs to climb up to the quarter. And as you always like to remind me, you have your blazer to protect you.'

'Corso! Damn you Corso, come back here!'

But he did not look back as he walked away across the blackened ruins of the lawn, even when I drew the blazer and blew a dead tree to splinters. I hoped that the shot might attract one of the killing machines that patrolled the city, but although I waited a full ten minutes, nothing stirred. At last, I climbed out of the airframe and began the long walk home.

Seven

Dev Veeder took my revelation more calmly than I had thought he would, even though I had taken the precaution of having arranged to meet with him in the presence of Colm Wardsmead, the nominal director of the diplomatic quarter and, therefore, of the entire city. Wardsmead was a shifty, self-satisfied man; although he liked to think of himself as a Medici prince, the effectiveness of his native cunning was limited by his laziness and contempt for others. I knew that Dev Veeder despised Wardsmead, but also knew that he would not dare lose control of his temper in the director's presence.

'This is all very awkward,' Wardsmead said, when I was done. 'Perhaps you would care to make a recommendation, Colonel Veeder. I am sure that you would want this matter handled discreetly.'

During my exposition, Dev Veeder had stood with his back to the egg-shaped room, looking out of the huge window towards the shaggy treetops of the parkland. Without turning around, he said, 'She's supposed to be doing research out there. It would be the best place for an arrest.'

'Away from the excitable gaze of the diplomatic community,' Wardsmead said. 'I quite understand, Colonel.'

He was unable to hide his satisfaction at Dev Veeder's discomfort. Veeder was a war hero and so difficult to discipline, but now Wardsmead believed that he had a stick with which to beat him.

Perhaps Veeder heard something he did not like in Wardsmead's tone. He turned and gave the man a hard stare and said, 'I always do what is best, Mr Wardsmead, not what is convenient. My men are tracking her as she makes her way back across the main dome. They will allow her to enter the back door to the quarter's parkland, and I will arrest her when she arrives.'

Wardsmead swung to and fro in the cradle of his chair, hands folded across his ample stomach, and said, 'I suppose the question is, once you have arrested her, has she done anything wrong?'

'Consorting with the enemy without permission is a crime,' Dev Veeder said promptly. 'Failing to reveal a weakness in the security of the diplomatic quarter is also a crime. Both are betrayals of trust.'

'Well, there we have it,' Wardsmead said.

'There will have to be a trial,' Dev Veeder told him.

'Oh, now, that would be an unnecessary embarrassment, don't you think? One of the shuttles is due to leave in a couple of days. We can ship her off –'

'There will be a trial,' Dev Veeder said. 'It is a security matter, and the crime was committed outside the diplomatic quarter, so it falls under martial law. She will be tried, and so will the old man.'

I said, 'You have arrested Yani Hakaiopulos?'

For the first time, Dev Veeder looked directly at me. I confess that I flinched. He said, 'The old man was not at the hospital, but there are only so many places he can hide. Your guide, the man Corso, has also vanished. I must assume that he is also part of the plot.'

I said, 'Yani Hakaiopulos was simply helping Demi understand how the parklands and wilderness had been put together. Surely that's not a crime?'

Using her first name was a mistake. Dev Veeder said coldly, 'You have admitted, Professor-Doctor Graves, that you did not know what they talked about. I have not arrested you only because stupidity is not a crime under either civil or martial law.'

Wardsmead said, 'I don't much care what happens to the two tweaks, but even if I allow you your trial, Colonel Veeder, I want an assurance that Dr Lacombe will be deported at the end of it.'

Despite his amiable tone, his forehead was greasy with sweat. He scented a scandal, and did not want its taint to sully his career.

Dev Veeder said, 'That depends on what I discover during my interrogation. And I can assure you, gentlemen, that it will be a very thorough interrogation. You will come with me, Professor-Doctor Graves.'

'I have already told you –'

'You will come with me,' Dev Veeder said again.

He wanted his revenge to be complete.

Eight

Camelot, Mimas fell; Baghdad, Enceladus fell; Athens and Spartica on Tethys surrendered within days of each other, blasted into submission by singleship attacks; the vacuum organism farms of Iapetus's carbonaceous plains were destroyed by viral infection; Phoebe, settled by the Redeemers, and the habitats which had remained in orbit around Titan, had all declared neutrality at the beginning of the war, and were under martial law.

Within two months of the arrival of the expeditionary force from Earth, the war was almost over. Only Paris, Dione remained defiant to the end. Singleships had taken out most of the city's peripheral installations. Its vacuum organism farms were dying. And now new stars flared in its sky as troop ships took up their eccentric orbits. The emergency committee of Paris voted to surrender, and the same night were assassinated by Marisa Bassi's followers. Bassi rallied the citizens, organised the barricades and the block captains, killed a party of negotiators in a fit of fury and killed his hostages too.

It was an unforgivable act, a terrible war crime, yet for Marisa Bassi and the citizens of Paris it was deeply

necessary. It was an affirmation of their isolation and their outlaw status. It united them against the rest of humanity.

I believe that Bassi was tired of waiting, tired of the slow attrition of the blockade. He was bringing the war right into the heart of his city and, like the people he led, was eager to embrace it.

Imagine that last day, as lights streaked across the sky as the troop ships launched their drop capsules. A battery of industrial X-ray lasers tried and failed to target them; a troop ship came over the horizon, pinpointed the battery, and destroyed it with a single low yield fission missile, stamping a new crater a kilometre wide on Remus crater's floor.

Marisa Bassi felt the shock wave of that strike as a low rumbling that seemed to pass far beneath the ground, like a subway train. He was in the street, organising the people who manned one of the barricades. It was mid-morning. He had been awake for more than forty-eight hours. His throat was sore and his lips were cracked. His eyes ached in their dry sockets and there was a low burning in his belly; he had drunk far too much coffee.

The scow had gone, and those citizens too old or too young to fight had been moved into the tunnels of the original colony. There was nothing left to do now but fight. The people knew this and seemed to be in good heart. They still believed that the Three Powers Alliance would not dare destroy their beautiful city, the jewel of the outer system, and perhaps Marisa Bassi believed it too. He felt that he carried the whole city in his heart, its

chestnut trees and cafés, trams and parklands, the theatre and the Bourse and the lovely glass cathedral, and he had never loved his adopted home as fiercely as he loved it now, in its last hours.

The barricade was in one of the service sectors near the perimeter of the dome, with diamond panes arching just above the rooftops of the offices and warehouses. It commanded a good view of a wide traffic circle, and on Bassi's orders men and women were cutting down stands of slim aspens to improve the fire lanes. Bassi was working with them, getting up a good sweat, when the tremor passed underneath. One of his young aides came running up, waving a TV strip like a handkerchief.

'They got the lasers,' she said breathlessly. She was fifteen or sixteen, almost twice Bassi's height, and trembled like a racehorse at the off. Like everyone else, she was wearing a pressure suit. The bowl of its helmet was hooked to her utility belt.

'We expected that,' Bassi said, staring up at her. He had shaved off his beard, cut his hair to within a millimetre of his scalp. His hands, grasping the shaft of his diamond-edged axe, tingled. He said, 'What else?'

'They're down,' the girl said, 'and coming along both ends of the ridge.'

'Any message from their command ship?'

'No sir.'

'And we won't send one. Get back to headquarters. Tell them I'll be back in twenty minutes.'

'Sir, shouldn't you –'

Bassi lifted the axe. 'I've a job to finish here. Go!'

They were mostly old men and women on that barricade, and knew that they would be among the first to engage the invaders. Why did Bassi stay with them? Perhaps he was exhausted. He had brought the whole city to this point by sheer force of will, and perhaps he saw nothing beyond the moment when the fighting started. Perhaps he knew then that defeat was inevitable, and wanted to make a last heroic gesture rather than face the ignominy of surrender.

In any case, he stayed. Once the aspens had been cleared, he went back with the others to the barricade. It was no more than a ridge of roadway that had been turned up by a bulldozer and topped with tangles of razor wire. They closed up the wire and started checking their weapons – machine pistols and blazers stamped out by a rejigged factory, an ungainly machine that used compressed air to fire concrete-filled cans.

Someone had a flask of brandy and they all took a sip, even Bassi's remaining aide. The flask was going around the second time when there was a brisk series of bangs in the distance, and a wind got up, swirling foliage broken from the aspens high into the air.

The invaders broke into the main dome of the city at nine points, breaching the basalt skirt with shaped charges, driving their transports straight through, and then spraying sealant to close the holes. At that point, they thought they could take the city without inflicting much damage.

While some of the people at the barricade latched up their helmets and checked their weapons, others were

still looking at TV strips. Bassi ripped the TVs from their hands, told them roughly to watch the street. The motor of the compressor gun started up with a tremendous roar and at the same moment sleek shining man-sized machines appeared on the far side of the traffic circle.

The killing things moved very quickly. It is doubtful that anyone got off a shot before the machines had crossed the traffic circle and leaped the razor wire. Bassi's aide ran, and a killing thing was on him in two strides, slicing and jabbing, throwing the corpse aside. The others were dispatched with the same quick ruthlessness, and then only Bassi was left, drenched in the blood of the men and women who had died around him, his arms and legs pinned by one of the killing things.

Once the barricade had been cleared, a squad of human troopers in sealed pressure suits came forward. Their sergeant photographed Bassi, cuffed him, and ordered one of his men to take him back for what he called a debriefing. Bassi knew then that he had been selected by chance, not because he had been recognised; shaving off his trademark beard had saved him. He smiled and spat on the sergeant's visor. The squad and the killing things moved on; the trooper marched Bassi at gunpoint across the traffic circle towards the command post at the breached perimeter.

No one knows how Bassi got free, only that he was captured at a barricade in the first minutes of fighting and then escaped. Certainly, he never reached the command post. Perhaps the trooper was killed by one of the snipers which infested the city, or perhaps Bassi got free on his

own; after all, he was a very resourceful man. In any case, it is known that he reached the Bourse two hours after the barricade fell, because he made a brief, defiant television transmission there.

I have watched this speech many times. It is the last sighting of him. He was wounded when he escaped, and the wound had been patched but the bullet was still inside him; he must have felt it, and felt the blood heavy and loose inside his belly as he spoke, but he showed no sign that he was in pain. He spoke for five minutes. He spoke clearly and defiantly, but it was a poor, rambling speech, full of allusions to freedom and idealism and martyrdom, and his steady gaze had a crazed, glittering quality.

By then, most of the outlying tents and domes of the city had been captured by the invaders; even Bassi's headquarters had been taken. The citizens of Paris had fallen back to the central part of the main dome. Most of the barricades had been overrun by killing things. Thousands of citizens lay dead at their posts, while the invaders had incurred only half a dozen casualties, mostly from snipers. The battle for Paris was clearly over, but still its citizens fought on.

'I warn the commander of the invaders,' Marisa Bassi said, 'that we will fight to the end. We will not let you take what we have built with our sweat and our blood. Paris will die, but Paris lives on. The war is not over.'

A few minutes later, the main buildings of the city were set on fire, filling the dome with smoke. A few minutes after that, the commander of the invasion force gave the order to breach the integrity of the main dome.

By then, no doubt, Bassi was already at one of the last barricades, armed with the carbine he had taken from the dead trooper, his pressure suit sealed. A great wind sucked fire and smoke from the burning, broken wedding cake of the Bourse; smoke rushed along the ground in great billows that thinned and vanished, leaving the eerie clarity and silence of vacuum. And then a shout over the radio, doubling and redoubling. Killing things were running swiftly across the wide lawns towards the last barricades, puffs of earth jumping around them as people started to fire.

Bassi drew himself up to face his enemy, no longer the leader of the free government of Paris, his fate no more significant now than any of the last of its citizens. He thought that he was only moments from death. He was wrong.

Nine

Demi Lacombe had stapled a nylon rope to a basalt outcrop at the edge of the mossy, emerald-green meadow; its blue thread fell away to the trough of black water a hundred metres below. Dev Veeder squatted on his heels and ran a gloved finger around the knot doubled around the eye of the staple, then looked up at me and said, 'I could loosen this so that she would fall as she climbed back up. Do you think the fall would kill her?'

'I think not. Not in this low gravity.'

He stood. 'No. I don't think so either. Well, she'll be here soon. We'd better keep out of sight.'

I dabbed sweat from my brow with the cuff of my shirt. I had been marched quickly through the parkland by Veeder's squad of troopers, as if I had been under arrest, with no chance until now of talking with him, of trying to change his mind. I said, 'Are you enjoying yourself, Colonel?'

'You want revenge too. Don't deny it. She used us both, Graves.'

'This seems so . . . melodramatic.'

'History is made with bold gestures. I want her arrested in the act of returning through a passageway which presents a clear and present danger to the security of the diplomatic community. I want you to be a witness.'

'No bold gesture can be based on so petty a motive as revenge.'

Dev Veeder moved closer to me, so close that when he spoke a spray of saliva fell on my cheek. 'We're in this together, Graves. Don't pretend that you're just an observer like that thing, DeHon. Be a man. Face up to the consequences of your actions.'

'She was only trying to do her work, Colonel. Your crazy jealousy got in the way –'

'We are both jealous men, Graves. But at least I did not betray her.'

Veeder shoved me away from him then, and I went sprawling on the soft, wet moss. By the time I had regained my feet, he was on the other side of the little meadow, showing the four troopers where to take cover. As they concealed themselves amongst the exuberant rose briars, the sergeant of the squad took me by the arm and pulled me into the shade of the ferns that cascaded down the basalt cliff.

It was hot and close inside the curtain of fern fronds. Sweat dripped from my nose, my chin, ran down my chest inside my shirt. Tiny black flies danced about my face with dumb persistence. In the meadow, huge, sulphur-yellow butterflies circled each other above the bright green moss, their hand-sized wings flapping once a minute. The sergeant, a muscular, dark-eyed woman,

hummed softly to herself, watching the screen she had spread on her knee. It showed a view of the lake below the meadow, transmitted from one of the tiny cameras the troopers had spiked here and there. Time passed. At last, the sergeant nudged me and pointed.

Centred in the screen, Demi Lacombe's silvery figure suddenly stood up, waist-deep, in black water. She stripped off her airmask and hooked it to her belt, waded to the gravelly shore and grasped the rope and swarmed up it, moving so quickly, hand over hand, that it seemed she was swimming through the air.

I looked up from the screen as she pulled herself over the edge of the meadow and rolled onto the vivid green moss. As she got to her feet, Dev Veeder stepped out of his hiding place, followed by his troopers; the sergeant shoved me roughly and I tumbled forward, landing on my hands and knees.

Demi looked at Dev Veeder, at me. For a moment I thought she might jump into the chasm, but then Dev Veeder crossed the meadow in two bounds and caught her by the left wrist, the one she had broken soon after arriving in Paris. She turned pale, and would have dropped to her knees if Dev Veeder had not held her up.

'All right,' he growled. 'All right.'

The brilliant light of the suspensor lamps hung high above dimmed. I felt a few fat rain drops on my face and hands, congealing rather than falling from the humid air.

The pathetic fallacy made real by Demi Lacombe's implants, I thought, and Dev Veeder must have had the same idea, because he said, 'Stop that, you bitch,' and

delivered a back-handed slap to her face while still
holding on to her wrist.

Demi's cry of pain was cut off by a roll of thunder; I
think I must have shouted out then, too, for the sergeant
grasped my arm and shook me and told me to shut the
fuck up. Those were her words. A sheet of sickly light
rippled overhead and the air darkened further as a wind
got up, blowing clouds of raindrops as big as marbles.
They hissed against the curtain of ferns above, and
drenched me to the skin in an instant.

Someone was standing at the edge of the rose thicket.

It was one of the gardeners. I was sure that it was the
one that Demi had summoned before – their shaven
heads and blank expression effaced individuality, but he
had the same stocky immigrant build and wary manner.
At his side was a pair of tawny panthers; a huge bird
perched on his upraised arms, its gripping claws digging
rivulets of bright blood from his flesh.

With a sudden snap, like playing cards dealt by a
conjuror, the four troopers formed a half circle in front
of Dev Veeder and Demi Lacombe. Their carbines were
raised. The rain was very thick now, blown up and down
and sideways by the gusting wind; water sheeted down
the closed visors of the troopers' helmets, the slick resin of
their chestplates.

The gardener made no move, but the panthers and
huge bird suddenly launched themselves across the
meadow. Two wild shots turned every drop of rain blood
red; the scream of air broken by their energy echoed off
the ferny cliff. Dev Veeder was struggling with Demi

Lacombe, a horrible, desperate waltz right at the edge of the cliff. One trooper was down, beating at the bird whose wings beat about his head; one of the panthers had bowled over two more troopers and the second took down a trooper as he fled. The trooper struggling with the bird took a step backwards, and fell from the edge of the meadow; a moment later, the bird rose up alone, wings spread wide as it rode the gust of wind that for a moment blew the rain clear of the meadow.

The sergeant raised her carbine. I saw that she had the presence of mind to aim at the gardener, and threw myself at her legs. The shot went wild. She kicked me hard and in the light gravity her legs flew from beneath her and she sat down. I fell flat on sodden moss, and was trying to unholster my blazer, although I do not know who I would have shot at, when the sergeant hauled me half-around by one of my arms – fracturing a small bone in my wrist, I later discovered – and struck my head with the stock of her carbine.

Then the bird fell upon her.

Ten

I was dazed and bloodied and far from the meadow when Lavet Corso found me. I did not remember how I had gotten away from the troopers – perhaps the gardener had led me to my former guide – nor did I remember seeing Dev Veeder and Demi Lacombe fall, but their drowned bodies were found a day later, lying together on a spit of gravel at the far end of the dark little lake, like lovers at the end of a tale of doomed romance. Although, of course, they were never lovers. Of that, at least, I am certain.

Corso told me that Demi Lacombe had been in the habit of using a pheromone-rich perfume to befuddle men from whom she wanted some favour or other. 'A kind of hypnotic,' Yani Hakaiopulos said. 'It does exactly what other perfumes only claim to do. He recognised it at once, and confirmed his suspicion using the hospital's equipment. He was amused at her presumption, and rather admired her ambition.'

We were crouched under the billowing skirts of a cypress, while the gale blew itself out around us. The gardener sat on his haunches a little way off, staring out into the rainy dark.

'Hakaiopulos wanted his gardens rebuilt,' I said dully. My head and wrist ached abominably, and I felt very cold.

Corso said, 'He'll get his chance, but not here. You know, you're a lucky man. Lucky that Veeder didn't kill you when he had the chance; lucky that I don't kill you now.'

'You should get away, Mr Corso. Go on: leave me. If Colonel Veeder finds you here –'

I did not know then that he was dead.

'I'm leaving Paris,' Corso said. 'I'm going to join my wife.'

For a moment, I thought he meant that he was going to kill himself. Perhaps he saw it in my face, because he added, 'She's not dead. None of the people who left on the scow are dead.'

'It fell into Saturn.'

'The scow did, yes. But before it took its dive, it travelled most of the way around the planet within the ring system, long enough to drop off its passengers and cargo in escape pods. There are millions of ice and rock bolides in the rings. Sure, most of them have been ground down to gravel and dust, but there's a sizeable percentage of bodies more than a couple of kilometres across – something like half a million.'

'This is fantasy, Mr Corso.'

'My wife and the other people who escaped have made their home on one of them; that's where I'm taking my daughter and a couple of other people. I would have gone sooner, but I had work to do here, and I couldn't justify the risk of stealing a shuttle until now.'

'You're saving Yani Hakaiopulos.'

'Him too. We can always use a gene wizard. But there's someone else, someone more important to us than anyone else.'

I said, 'It was you who painted those slogans, wasn't it? You could move freely about the city because you smell right to the killing machines. *He lives*. Another silly fantasy, Mr Corso. He died with the fools he was leading.'

Corso shook his head. 'After he escaped, he made his way back to the main dome and rallied the last of the barricades. We still thought then that if enough soldiers died while attempting to take Paris, we might carry the day. We were giving our lives for the city, after all, but the soldiers were dying for no more than the redemption of a loan. But you sent in killing machines, and then you blew the dome. Like most of the people at the barricades, Marisa Bassi was wearing a pressure suit, and he continued to fight until he ran out of air. In his last moments of consciousness he hid amongst the dead who lay all around him. The suit saved his life by chilling him down, but lack of oxygen had already caused brain damage. After one of the corpse details found him, he was carefully resuscitated, but his frontal lobes were badly damaged. The implants keep him functioning, and one day we'll be able to reconstruct him.'

You have to understand that although this was the most fantastic part of Corso's story, it is the part I believe without question, for I insisted on examining the gardener myself. His hands were strong and square, with blunt fingers, yes, but so are the hands of most labourers.

But I also saw the wound in his side, just under his ribs, the wound he suffered when he escaped, a wound into which I could insert my smallest finger.

Corso took me as far as the edge of the parkland, and I do not know what became of him – or of his daughter, or Yani Hakaiopulos, or the gardener, Marisa Bassi. A shuttle was stolen during the confusion after Colonel Veeder's death, and was later found, abandoned and gutted, in an eccentric orbit that intersected the ring system.

As for myself, I have decided not to return to Earth. There are several colonies which managed to remain neutral during the Quiet War, and I hope to find a place in one of them. The advance of my fee should be sufficient to buy citizenship. I once planned to endow a chair of history in my name, as a snub to my rivals, but using the credit to win a new life, if only for a few years, now seems a better use for it.

I hope that they will be peaceful years. But before he left me to my grief and to my dead, Lavet Corso told me that his was not the only clandestine colony hidden within the ring system's myriad shifting orbits, and his last words still make me shiver.

'The war's not over.'